BAD

PEOPLE

Kim Ulrick

Contempo Publishing

652 Hogans Rd North Tumbulgum NSW 2490.
www.contempopublishing.com
Copyright © Kim Ulrick 2026.

A catalogue entry for this book is available from the National Library of Australia.

ISBN (Paperback):   978 1 7643986 8 8
ISBN (eBook):   978 1 7643986 9 5

Cover design and illustration by Rubi Creations Digital.
Internal design by Contempo Publishing.

Printed and distributed internationally by Ingram Spark.

First published in 2026 by Contempo Publishing.

In the spirit of reconciliation, I acknowledge the traditional custodians of country throughout Australia and their connections to land, sea and community. I pay respect to elders past, present and emerging, and extend that respect to all Aboriginal and Torres Strait Islander peoples.

This book is a product of my imagination, creativity and countless hours of hard work. It was crafted with love, passion and dedication. Rest assured that this book was not generated by any artificial intelligence. It's a testament to the human spirit and the joy of storytelling.

Trigger Warning

This book contains scenes that may depict, mention or discuss hauntings, abduction, violence, death, human trafficking, sexual abuse and stalking.

For the thin blue line.

The men and women who face the worst in humanity

and risk their lives every day to protect ours.

Prologue

Blinking, she tries to pierce the thick blanket of darkness that envelops her.

Panic edges its way into her clouded brain as she realises she's spreadeagled across a bed. Her wrists are tied and her ankles bound.

Silky sheets rub against her skin as she struggles with the bindings. Tape has been stuck over her mouth, so when she calls for help, all that escapes is a muffled whimper.

A door opens and light streams in. A man enters the room; he's wearing a mask, and as he leans over and tucks her hair behind her ears, his face hovers mere centimetres from her breasts. The smell of cheap aftershave and sweat is overpowering.

She twists away, yanks against the ropes, trying to free herself.

'Let's get a better look at you,' he coos as she thrashes around on the mattress. 'Aren't you a cutie?' Bony fingers dig into her cheeks and he turns her face to his. 'Now, sweetheart, behave and show everyone how lovely you are.'

A soft glow illuminates her skin as he sweeps a phone up her legs to her torso and chest, recording every angle of her body.

She shies away from the camera, and he chuckles, 'You really are a live wire, aren't you? I have something that can help with that.'

A sharp pain pierces her arm. The darkness returns.

Chapter 1

His huge, tattooed frame has been squeezed into the driver's seat of his Mustang. He drums his fingers on the steering wheel in time to the pumping beats reverberating from the speakers and waits, glancing at his phone and huffing in frustration.

Tommo is one of his regular, most reliable buyers, but somehow he's always late.

Dan has parked in a dingy corner of the shopping centre basement, as far as possible from the main entrance and its security cameras. His windows are heavily tinted, hiding him from prying eyes, but it pays to be careful.

Careful or not, he's so engrossed in the music that he jumps when the passenger door opens and a tall man wearing low-slung baggy pants and a hoodie slides into the seat beside him.

'What took you so long?' he grunts, regaining his composure.

'Why? You on a tight schedule, Tiny?'

No one in his network calls him Dan.

'I have shit to do,' he grumbles as he pulls a bag of white powder from his glove box. Pushing his irritation to one side, he switches to sales mode. 'It's a good cut. Quality stuff.'

Tommo leans over, dips his pinkie finger into the powder and snorts it off. He leans back in the seat and closes his eyes before responding. 'Mmm … it's good. How much you asking?'

'Seven.'

'Bit steep.'

'Steep or not, that's what it costs.'

Tommo shrugs and hands over the cash. As Dan checks it, he rehearses in his head what he's about to say.

'You said some chicks are gonna be on the market soon,' he says as casually as he can manage. 'I have buyers, I just need to know who to talk to.'

'Man, you don't wanna get involved,' Tommo replies, eyes widening in alarm. 'Trust me. I heard the crew behind it … steer clear. Don't mess with 'em.'

'Yeah, but if I can hook these guys up, the payout will be sweet. Help me out.' Dan pulls a small bag of tablets from his pocket and lays them, tantalisingly, in his lap. Tommo could never resist a freebie. 'I'll throw these in. Payment for the tip off.'

'Alright,' Tommo says, snatching up the bag and shoving it into the pocket of his hoodie. 'I mean, I'm not your mother, right?'

Dan says nothing. Waits.

'All I know is you have to go through some old dude. Don't know his name, but I know how you can reach him.'

Dan reaches into the glove box and pulls out a pen and an old napkin. He hands them to Tommo, who scribbles down the details, opens the car door and almost sprints away. Dan watches him disappear through the exit, towards the nearby train station, then starts the car and pulls away.

Driving home, Dan weighs up what to do. If he tells the cops about this, he can never go back. He'll be marked as a snitch forever. Perhaps he could say Tommo lied, that he was big noting himself and didn't have any useful info. He could take the hit from the cops, do his time instead.

But as he pulls up outside his place, his phone buzzes. It's his mum, sending him a video of his baby girl giggling at the camera. And that's when he realises he has no choice.

There's a tawny frogmouth hidden in the branches of the gum tree on the front lawn, and Leading Senior Constable Erica Martin has gotten used to its familiar *oom-oom* noise whenever she gets home. It's like her own little welcoming committee. She unlocks the front door of the Federation bungalow she and her partner Simon share, drops her bag in the bedroom, and heads straight for the shower. When she's done, she wraps her hair in a towel – her strawberry blonde tresses damp and darkened – dons a dressing gown and picks up her laptop before making her way to the kitchen.

No time off for you, Erica, she thinks. *No wonder I look so tired.*

She remembers Simon pulling her up on this just a day or two back: 'You need to make time for yourself. You can't give every minute of your life to this job, you know.' He has a point, but she is determined to prove herself. The DC has given her an opportunity not many officers of her rank or younger age have had before – leading a specialist team on a high-profile taskforce and reporting directly to one of the most experienced assistant commissioners on the force. She doesn't want to stuff it up.

Besides, she thinks to herself, Simon's job is even more demanding. As a doctor in the final year of his rotations and training at Parramatta District Hospital, when Simon isn't doing double shifts, he's being called in on his days off because they're short-staffed. He tries not to bring work home like she does, but she can always tell if it's been a tough day from how quiet he is after his shift.

Yawning, she pulls a small lasagne from the freezer before popping it in the microwave and pouring herself a glass of pinot. When the oven pings, she slips the heated pasta onto a plate, perches on a stool at the island bench, and gets to work.

First job is to log on to Taskforce Lacuna's secure site and check her messages. There's one from her boss, Assistant Commissioner Sam Stirling, linking to a TV interview with Deputy Commissioner Robyn Jones, which aired earlier that evening. Erica clicks through, and the segment begins with a female reporter standing in front of the NSW Police Headquarters in Parramatta, holding a photo of a woman.

'Two years on, the search for 21-year-old Sydney woman Ally Webster continues and the police have issued a new plea for anyone with information to come forward, with the posting of a $500,000 reward for anyone who has genuine information related to her disappearance.

'But while Ally is the focus of this latest announcement, over the last few months there has been a concerning increase in the number of young women who've gone missing in suspicious circumstances across the state. In response, the NSW Police have set up a new specialist squad – Taskforce Lacuna – to investigate these unexplained disappearances.'

The footage cuts to Deputy Commissioner Jones in full uniform. She's sitting in an armchair in a wood-panelled office, the reporter sitting opposite and listening intently.

'Ally Webster was last seen exiting Heathcote train station in the Sutherland Shire on the evening of Friday, 3 February 2023. We believe someone in the community has vital information about Ally's movements on the night she was last seen, and possibly, what happened to her. Every hour, every day that she is missing is an hour and a day too long for her family.'

'You've set up a new missing persons' taskforce,' the reporter says. 'Can you tell us what prompted you to dedicate additional resources to this now?'

'On average, 28 people go missing every day in New South Wales,' Jones begins. 'While the majority of them are found within a few days or weeks of their disappearance, about one per cent go on to be long-term missing people – individuals who've been missing for more than 90 days. What we are particularly concerned about, however, is the high number of young women who have disappeared in suspicious circumstances in the last few months – five in total. That represents a highly unusual increase, and that's why we've established Taskforce Lacuna to prioritise our investigation into these cases.'

The footage cuts to a middle-aged woman at a dining table in a kitchen that looks like it hasn't been renovated since the 80s. She's holding a photo of a young woman – Ally – cradling a puppy. 'Meanwhile, Ally's mother, Peta Webster, says she will never stop searching for her daughter.'

'Living life without my beautiful girl has been the most difficult pain I've ever had to endure,' Mrs Webster says, barely holding back her tears. 'And I feel for those other families who are going through what we've experienced. I know the police are doing their best, but I keep hoping someone out there has information that can help us find Ally so we can bring her home.'

The camera cuts back to the reporter. 'Anyone with any information is urged to call Crimestoppers –'

Erica closes the media player. Until now, Taskforce Lacuna has been operating under the radar but increasing pressure from the premier, police minister and numerous women's and victims' rights groups has forced them to show that action is being taken.

And maybe she has the breakthrough they're all crying out for.

She's spent weeks cultivating trust and a relationship with Dan Garfield, a huge brute of a man connected to the Scorpions bikie gang. Slowly, she's been persuading him to act as a source, an informant for the police in exchange for witness protection.

Garfield is a single father, and Erica has offered a new life for him, his baby daughter and his mother, who's helping to care for his child.

And tonight, Garfield called to tell her he now had contact details of a possible human trafficker. Someone who might lead her to one or more of the five missing Australians she's searching for.

Her phone pings: it's Simon.

HELLO BEAUTIFUL. HOPE YOU HAD A GOOD DAY. TRY TO GET SOME SLEEP TONIGHT. YOU'LL BE GONE BEFORE I GET HOME.
LOVE YOU AND MISS YOU.

The light from the brass pendant above the bench reflects off the wine glass as she twirls the stem and smiles at his message. She was nervous about moving in with him after only a few months of dating, but now she's sure it was the right move. Their demanding jobs and long hours mean they make the most of every moment they spend together.

Grinning, she taps out a quick reply.

I'M STILL UP. HAD A LONG DAY BUT SUCCESSFUL.
HOPE YOUR'E WINNING TOO.
LOVE E.

By now, the wine has had the desired effect, and Erica's eyes are drooping, so she places her dirty plate and glass in the dishwasher and falls into the king bed. She's asleep in an instant.

Chapter 3

Laura and Ki are last in line. Red blotches creep up her neck to her cheeks as she watches her competitors complete the punishing course.

They've faced some tough challenges together and have already built a reputation as a formidable team, but somehow the Australasian Police Dog Games are making her more nervous than all of those put together. It's the first time the games have been held in five years, thanks to the COVID pandemic and dwindling budgets, but now they've been reinstated as a biennial event, with teams from across Australia and New Zealand taking part. This year, the event is on Laura's home turf – Campbelltown Oval, southwest of Sydney – but that doesn't reduce her adrenaline any. Perhaps it's the crowds; the games have become immensely popular for spectators, offering magic photo opportunities.

In an era where every police force is struggling for recruits, it's brilliant PR.

Ki, her black German Shepherd – and, she has no trouble admitting, her best friend – whimpers as he leans against her leg.

He plants his paw on her foot, seeking reassurance, and Laura rubs his ears as she closes her eyes and visualises the two of them moving through each obstacle and task. By the time the head of the NSW Police Canine Training Unit, Sergeant Tyler, calls them forward, both handler and dog are calm and focused.

The whistle blows and Laura releases Ki, running alongside him as he clambers over the agility course. They make great time, until the final hurdle, an enormous fence Ki must climb as quickly as possible. It's this obstacle that causes Laura the most stress. Each time in practice Ki has taken several attempts to get over, and to do that now would cost them the competition. But her partner scrambles over it with ease, racing to the finish line without breaking stride. Laura joins him, scuffing his ears and pulling him in for a cuddle and play as they wait for their time to flash up on the screen.

The crowd, including her parents and grandfather Jack, erupts with cheers.

They're the fastest team.

Ki has already defended Laura against a knife-wielding attacker in the previous round, leaping to her defence, growling and disarming the aggressor before pinning him to the ground. All that remains is the tracking challenge.

When the time comes, Laura places a piece of clothing under Ki's nose and gives him the command to find. He sniffs this way and that, his muzzle close to the ground while he moves in a widening circle, then he zooms off toward the stadium's stands, leaving Laura sprinting to keep up on the other end of his long lead.

Ki stops, ears up and alert, and Laura almost barrels into him, then, snarling, he launches himself at a row of empty seats. His quarry breaks cover, leaping over the fence and sprinting across the oval, with Ki barking and giving chase. Fast as the man is running, he stands no chance – the dog knocks the mock criminal to the ground and then stands guard over him as Laura handcuffs and then leads him away.

Pulling a rope toy from her jacket, Laura plays tug of war with Ki while commending him on a job well done.

The gold medal is heavier than Laura thought it would be, although Ki doesn't seem bothered about the one he wears around his neck. She stands there with a goofy smile as her parents and grandfather fuss around her, and for a moment, she imagines her Gran with them. The pull and memory are so strong that she can even smell rosewater, her grandmother's favourite perfume. Since she'd passed, Laura has felt Gran's presence. Sometimes it catches her off guard, hitting her at random moments, like when she's watching TV or listening to music but it's particularly powerful in this moment.

Her diminutive mother puts her arms around Laura, and murmurs in her ear, 'Well done, sweetheart, we're so proud of you,' then passes her to her towering father and her grandfather Jack, who each take their turn dragging her into bear hugs.

As she poses for more pictures, Laura spots a familiar face in the crowd. Five years ago, she and Erica Martin had bonded during the search for a missing teenager. Back then, Erica had been just a cadet who Laura's family had put up in their home during the investigation, but the strong friendship and respect they had for each other had remained long after and had propelled Laura to apply to the force.

For Laura, to have her old friend share in her moment of triumph was icing on the cake.

'You won!' Erica says as she pumps Laura's hand. 'I knew you could do it!'

'Thanks. I can't believe it. It doesn't feel real.'

'I never doubted you,' Erica crows.

'So how come you're here?' Laura asks. 'I'd have thought they'd be keeping you too busy for something like this.'

'Wouldn't miss it,' Erica replies. 'But I did need to chat with Sergeant Tyler about something, too.' She gives Laura a look that twinkles with mischief.

'What?' Laura asks, swamped with curiosity.

'I'm not sure if you realise,' Erica says, 'but as competition winner, you can request a new assignment if you want to.'

'I had heard something like that.'

'Good. Because I have a proposition for you. How would you like to be temporarily assigned to my team on Taskforce Lacuna?'

'Seriously?' Laura asks. 'I could do that?' The taskforce, with its remit to investigate the rash of missing women, was big news at the moment—getting assigned to it would be massive!

'I'm confident I could get you a secondment. We've only been going for a little while but I lost one of my team members recently and I don't know when, or even if, he'll be back. So, I need more help, plus you've got great instincts. I could use you and Ki to go over old ground and see if you can pick up any scents or clues we've missed.'

'Would there be enough work for us?'

'I'm sure there'll be heaps! But if you're worried, I can set up a sharing arrangement with your boss at Sutherland. It'll give you time to work out where you want to go next.'

'That would be … fantastic! Thanks, Erica.'

'Brilliant. I'll make some calls and message you later.'

And by the time Erica wanders away through the crowd, Laura has completely forgotten about the medal around her neck.

Chapter 4

Ki dozes in his crate in the back of the car as Laura weaves through early morning traffic to her new job in Parramatta. Only in Sydney could there be this many cars on the road at 6.30 am.

By the time she arrives at the offices of Taskforce Lacuna, Erica is already waiting for them in the foyer with her access pass to the building. Directing her into the elevator – Ki trotting alongside and drawing smiles from other staff in the building – Erica swipes her own card to activate the keypad and pushes the button for the third floor.

'It's a pretty small team,' she explains as the car jolts them upwards. 'Multi-disciplinary but focused on surveillance and intelligence gathering. You're one of several people we have working on short-term secondment.'

She leads Laura into a vacant office with more than enough space for her and Ki. The name on the door says *Detective Richard Ryan*, and boxes of files are stacked all over.

'There'll be a briefing later when I'll introduce you to everyone,' Erica says, 'but let's set you up here for now. I'd like you to review the case files for each woman first, get you up to speed.'

'Is Detective Ryan the team member you lost?' Laura asks.

Erica nods soberly. 'He had a stroke, a big one. He's only in his mid-30s and is pretty fit, so it came as a massive shock to everyone. Completely out of the blue. Right now, I've got no one else for the critical analysis of facts and evidence. We'll pull another detective from their current duties eventually, but in the meantime, I really need someone to bring the threads together for me.'

'Happy to help,' Laura says.

Erica grins. 'Once you're across all the information, contact the officers at each location to discuss the cases in more detail. If it's possible, I'd like you to take Ki out to the places where the women went missing, too. See if you can dig up any new clues.'

It takes Laura most of the day to get through all the material. While the case notes are clear and thorough, they're unfinished, beyond Detective Ryan concluding there was no clear pattern to the abductions. The women disappeared from all over NSW – Sydney, Newcastle, Armidale, Leeton – with the only consistent element that they were all young, the oldest being 24-years-old.

Interviews with family members, friends and colleagues all said the same thing — that the women taking off was out of character. Meanwhile, there have been no withdrawals from bank accounts, no calls and no traces at all of their whereabouts from phones or other devices.

The youngest woman to vanish, Laura read, is Sophie Romano, 18-years-old and still living at home. From her photo in the file, she is pretty and petite with olive skin and chocolate-brown eyes framed by wavy dark hair. Her family comes from old money and are well-respected in their home community of Leeton, having lived and farmed there for generations.

An aspiring actor and singer, Sophie attended a Catholic co-ed school, where she'd thrown herself into school plays, musicals and local theatre productions. She had even landed herself a regular gig entertaining diners at a nearby winery.

Her car was found on a lonely stretch of gravel road on the outskirts of town, far from home and the winery, and in a spot covered by neither CCTV nor traffic cameras. A forensic examination of her vehicle did not yield any clues.

One sunny Sunday morning, Sophie got in her car to drive to a gig at the vineyard. She never showed up.

Moving to the next case, Laura starts reading about Meg Harrison, 21-years-old and a registered nurse at Parramatta District Hospital. The photo in this file shows a curvaceous blonde with almond-shaped blue eyes, the various interviews with friends describing a popular woman who is the life of the party. The same friends also talked about a messy break-up she'd been through with a man they described as the 'jealous type', but that had been a few months before she disappeared. More than that, detectives had tracked down the ex and found he wasn't even in Australia – he was backpacking through Europe.

Meg lived close to the hospital and often walked to work, by no means a long trip. On the last night she was seen, she had been rostered on for the evening shift, but she never arrived.

The next file Laura picks up is on Cassie Brighton, 19, from Newcastle. An admin officer for an accounting firm, she'd enrolled into Business Studies at TAFE, with plans to become a qualified accountant. She was a volunteer lifesaver at Nobbie's Beach and regularly competed in Ironwoman competitions. Cassie, the file reads, had custody of her younger brother Josh following the sudden death of their mother, and was devoted to her sibling; her friends said she'd never leave him. Yet after dropping Josh at high school in the morning, she never collected him.

The fourth missing woman is Tori Engel, a 20-year-old dance teacher from Armidale with a part-time job pulling beers. Working at a historic pub that had been newly renovated as a popular hangout for students at the nearby University of New England, Tori is well-known to many locals, as is her ambition to open a dance studio. Laura studies her picture – a tall, red-haired, blue-eyed woman with a dazzling smile – and understands how the missing woman could be so well liked. Like the others, Tori just disappeared. She was on her way from the busy lunch shift at the pub to teach a dance class.

The fifth file covers the oldest woman to vanish, 24-year-old Siobhan Kennedy. A social worker with the NSW government, she helped place at-risk children in foster care, and Laura doesn't need to have a psychology degree to recognise what led the young woman to that particular path. Siobhan's father was convicted of murdering her mother when she was 12, then took his own life in prison, leaving Siobhan to be shunted from home to home until she finally ended up with a loving foster family who helped her deal with her traumatic childhood. In her file photo, Siobhan beams as she holds up her Diploma of Counselling; with dark-blonde, shoulder-length hair, blue eyes and dimples, she's good-looking but it's her smile that makes her beautiful, lighting up her face.

Siobhan was last seen on her day off, leaving for her regular walk to a park near her home in Fairfield. Footage from a security camera facing the street from the house she shares with three friends, shows her clutching a book in one hand and a water bottle in the other as she strolls along the footpath. She wasn't seen again.

There's one file left to tackle, and Laura gets up from her seat, her spine cracking as it straightens out from hunching over the papers. Still standing, she flips open the folder before pulling the notes toward her.

'What the …?' she exclaims to herself.

She hadn't expected to find Ally Webster – almost a cold case now – in with these recent reports. Why had Detective Ryan pulled her case and placed it among them?

But Laura is also thrown by the presence of the file because Ally's disappearance was one of the first investigations she'd ever worked on.

She had been a new constable, stationed at Heathcote, when she met Mrs Webster, long before starting her role as a dog handler. She and her senior partner had interviewed the distraught mother the day after Ally failed to return home from classes, where she'd been training as a vet. It had been Laura who had lodged the missing person's report; she'd never dreamed Ally would still be missing all these years later, and that she, Laura, would be part of a taskforce investigating her disappearance.

There's a soft knock on the door, and Laura looks up, grateful for the interruption. 'Come in.'

A young man opens the door and peers inside. Laura caught a glimpse of him while Erica led her through the office earlier that morning, and she'd assumed he was one of the team. Decked out in jeans, a retro Space Invaders t-shirt and Nike sneakers, up close, he looks like he'd be happier at home playing *Fortnite* or *Call of Duty*.

'Um … Senior Constable Murray, I'm doing a coffee run and wondered if you wanted one?'

'That would be awesome,' she replies, and walks around the desk, hand extended. 'But please, call me Laura.'

The man edges through the doorway and takes her hand; his fingers are cool, and his grip firm. 'Leon Campbell,' he says, as Ki rises from his spot and inches forward to greet the visitor.

'And this is Police Dog Ki.'

Leon crouches and Ki hold up his paw for a shake. 'You're smart, aren't you?'

Ki barks in agreement.

'Don't give him a big head,' Laura jokes. 'He just won gold at the Police Dog Games, and he's been unbearable.'

Leon's skin crinkles around the corners of his eyes when he laughs, and Laura becomes all too aware of the long, dark, curly lashes that frame his hazel eyes. His well-trimmed beard hides a baby face, and she guesses he's only a little older than her 25 years.

'Look, do you mind if we come with you?' she finds herself asking before she can stop herself. 'Ki is due for a break and I need to find out where to go.'

'Sure,' Leon smiles and pats Ki while Laura packs the sensitive documents away and locks the office. 'I prefer the coffee at Stefano's. It's a bit of a trek, but worth the effort.'

They detour through the park on the way back, to exercise Ki, sipping their coffees, as they walk. For someone she's literally just met, Laura finds Leon surprisingly easy to talk to, and by the time they're back at the office they've covered everything from coffee preferences to fitness routines. Laura even finds herself telling him that she's training for the next City-to-Surf fun run, a fact she's shared with no one else yet.

'You're a runner, hey?'

'Every day,' she replies. 'Helps having the Royal National Park backing onto my house.'

'Can't say I've ever been a fan of pounding the pavement. I'm not the overly sporty type, but I go to the gym a few times a week to stay fit.' Laura checks out his appearance again, and this time she notices well-toned biceps pushing against the sleeves of his t-shirt. 'To be honest, I'd rather spend the time gaming or on my guitar, but I believe in the old mantra – healthy body, healthy mind.'

'Nice. My sister's a bit of a muso, too. Keyboards.'

'And yourself?'

Laura smiles. 'Not so much.'

As the lift doors open, they step into the car and Leon swipes them up for the third floor.

'Thanks,' she says as they rise up through the building.

'For what?'

'Taking a newbie to the best coffee spot. Maybe we can do it again?' she suggests and hides her smile by sipping from her cup.

Chapter 5

The late afternoon sun flickers through the leaves of the gum trees as the crimson heads of towering Gymea lilies bob in the southerly breeze. The gentle wind is a reprieve from the heat that rises from the ground, sucking the air from Laura's lungs.

She stops for a drink, sweat dripping down her face as she pauses the app on her watch, and after getting her breath back, she continues her attack on the dirt track to the headland. Legs pumping, she forces herself to keep up a cracking pace, huffing as the path rises before her.

By the time she reaches the lookout, she's panting hard, and has to bend over to draw air into her chest. She stops her watch, recording her time, then wanders to the edge of the cliff, sucking down more water as she goes. As she stretches her muscles and admires the view, she inhales briny air redolent of oysters, the wind gusting off the sea lifting the end of her auburn ponytail, which flicks back and forth like a snake about to strike. Ahead of her, sparkling water stretches out to meet a cloudless sky, white caps dotting the ocean like they've been dabbed on by a painter.

Crunching footsteps tell her she's not alone. Deep, rasping breaths behind her indicating that a man has also conquered the challenging track to take in the postcard vista.

She moves back from the edge, turns to say hello, and her water bottle crashes to the ground, the clear liquid turning red as it soaks into the dirt. Her scream sticks in her throat, reduced to a strangled gurgle.

'I said you'd never be free of me,' says the man who haunted her teenage dreams. He steps closer and touches her cheek. 'My top-shelf prize.' He sighs. 'If only.'

Laura slaps his hand away. 'You're dead!' she yells. 'You can't hurt me!'

'No. But then, I'm not the only one who wants to.'

'What's that supposed to mean?'

'You'll find out.' He chuckles as he backs away, dissolving into the long shadows cast by the trees. 'I'll be seeing you, sweet thing.'

Laura jumps as if she's been scalded, scattering pillows to the floor, her heart pumping so hard she can feel it pounding from behind her ribs.

'Shadow Man,' she whispers into the night.

Switching on the lamp, she gathers up and rearranges the pillows before pulling open the top drawer of the bedside cabinet.

She rifles through socks and underwear before pulling out a leatherbound book and cradling it to her.

Her dream journal.

She flips through accounts she's recorded on its pages. In the past, they've revealed secrets or warned of imminent danger. Words and phrases leap out at her, and she pauses over an early entry. Her fingers trace the messy handwriting, and she pictures a frightened, younger version of herself crouched over the journal in the dark, using the light on her phone to record her dream.

Shadow Man was in the doorway again last night. That's the second time this week. He didn't show his face. He never does. He hides in shadows, shrouded in darkness. He scares me. He doesn't speak. I feel like he wants me. Wants to HURT me. I woke up before he could get me.

Laura's breathing quickens as she turns to a later extract, fear and anxiety flooding back as she relives it.

Last night I dreamt of the gorge. I tried to save the convict and baby before they were thrown from the cliff. But HE heard me. I turned and finally saw his face. He's the man who stopped me to ask for directions today. HE IS THE SHADOW MAN. Then everything shifted. Morphed. I was hiding under a blanket in the back seat of a car. The road was rough and when we stopped he took a kayak off the roof. I could hear water lapping the shore and then he dragged something heavy out of the back of his ute. He saw me, pointed, and said I was next.

She turns to the back of the book, where she has stuffed a wad of old newspaper clippings and pulls them out. She spreads the articles on top of the doona. One headline screams -

Australia's most-feared serial killer in custody

The article describes how police raided the home of a miner in Laura's hometown of Wallaby Rock. Gary Wilson – whom the press had dubbed the Bush Basher – had evidence on his property linking him to four murders, including those of Benny and Jordy Thompson, the younger brothers of Laura's best friend, Joanna.

What the article didn't say was that Gary had chosen Laura as his next victim, and that she had given police the breakthrough they needed by telling them of a strange encounter with Gary and her disturbing dreams. As a teenager, Laura's sleep had been haunted by the Shadow Man, but it was only when he'd laid a trap to kidnap her – a trap that failed when her best friend Joanna turned up – that she'd realised the Shadow Man was Gary Wilson.

It was Erica, staying with Laura's family during the search for Gary's fourth victim, Mia Stevens, who had believed in Laura's dreams and pushed for her senior officers to take the teenager's visions and her statement seriously. If Erica hadn't supported her, Laura may have become the next trophy in Gary's gruesome collection. As it was, Laura led them to the discovery of Mia, whose body was found in a nearby lake.

Ultimately, her testimony helped put the brutal killer in prison, where his life ended after a violent confrontation with another inmate.

She pulls out the pen she keeps tucked into the spine of the journal and records what she has dreamt tonight. Then, replacing the pen and newspaper articles, she closes the cover, shutting out the past.

'I won't let you win,' she vows to herself before returning the journal to its drawer.

Flicking off the light, she pulls the doona tight around her.

Chapter 6

Erica watches from the surveillance van as Dan Garfield heaves himself onto the top step of the tiny porch. Sweat trickles down his face and onto his muscle shirt, which is stretched so tight across his chest that he looks like a sausage about to burst its skin. He raps on the door, and through the pinhole camera in his baseball cap, Erica can see the word PURE inked across his knuckles.

The rattle of a train shakes the weatherboard home and echoes from her source's microphone to her ears. The door opens, and muted notes of classical music become audible on the line.

Dan leans into the small gap and whispers, 'Blackjack is my favourite game,' and the door swings open in response to the magic words, like the entrance to Aladdin's secret cave.

Erica inches forward, her nose almost touching the small screen in front of her. 'Show yourself,' she breathes, and sure enough, as Garfield ambles sideways into the house, she catches a glimpse of the person she's been chasing.

'Gotcha,' she cries, fist-pumping the air. 'Did you get that?' she asks the young technician sitting in front of her.

'You bet,' Leon says, his smile wide.

'Send that to your guys, get them to run him through facial recognition, see if we get a ping. And turn up the sound on the microphone.'

'On it,' Leon replies before whispering instructions to their source.

Erica fiddles with her headphones and pops a piece of chewing gum into her mouth, observing the interactions of the two men through the hidden camera.

The suspect Erica's been pursuing leads the way through the tiny, rundown house, taking a seat on a leather couch so large that it dominates the small lounge room it's been placed in. Tossing two cushions to one side, he motions to Dan, 'Park it.'

Lowering himself onto the lounge, Dan cracks his knuckles and surveys the room, giving Erica a full sweep of the space. Turning to face the older man, he says, 'My clients are interested in your product, but they want a sample.'

The other man laughs, smooths down his wispy grey hair. 'What do you think this is, a bloody delicatessen? Don't waste my time. You want in, say so. Otherwise …' He starts to rise from the lounge.

'Okay, but what about some images?' Dan presses. 'To show what you have? They want to make sure the product is up to scratch.'

Erica nods and whispers to herself, 'Yes. Good stuff. Keep pushing.'

The contact lowers himself to the couch again. 'Pictures aren't free. It'll cost you. What are they looking for?'

Dan shuffles on the couch, looks down, and Erica catches sight of legs like tree trunks, skimpy gym shorts riding up as his skin sticks to the leather. 'Under 25. Blonde, brunette or redhead, doesn't matter. They'll pay big dollars but they have to be top quality. No junkies or washed-up hookers.'

'Twenty grand buys you a few minutes of screen time … to prove I'm a man of my word. Cash up front.'

'Too easy. How's it works then? How do they get access?'

'Cash first, then I'll tell you.'

'Can they talk to the girls as well?'

The older man snorts. 'Not for 20k. But they'll get a taste of what's on offer and believe me, that's generous.'

Dan nods, the image on Erica's screen bobbing up and down with the motion. 'Okay,' he says, standing. 'I'll be in touch.'

'Not so fast,' the dealer snaps. 'Need to know who I'm dealing with here. I don't know your real name or who you represent. You said you heard about me through one of your buyers, but I'm the one sticking my neck out here, so I want credentials.'

'Like I said before, I'm Tiny. And trust me, my clients are rock solid.' There's a pause, as he stares at the contact, and Erica wonders what he's doing.

Whatever it is, it has the desired reaction.

'Well, why didn't you just say so,' the older man says. 'That'll do nicely.

Chapter 7

Laura looks from the folder in front of her, up at the image of the suspect on the briefing room screen. She shivers. There's something disconcerting about knowing the man they're tracking lives in Heathcote too, only a few kilometres across the railway tracks from her.

He reminds her of a senior citizen at a bingo parlour, but she's learned not to underestimate what human beings are capable of. She's had firsthand experience of how bad people can be, how rotten to the core. This innocent-looking, greying old bloke with a receding hairline and comb over could be a key player in the disappearance of half a dozen women. And to be honest, the thought she has unwittingly gone about her daily life so close to him makes her skin crawl.

'Our suspect's name is Cain Anderson,' Erica says, addressing her assembled team. 'He's 68 and did time for violent sexual offences in the 90s. He's never been a fully-fledged member of the Scorpions but has connections to some prominent members of the outlaw motorcycle gang. When our informant flashed him his scorpion tattoo, Anderson couldn't bend over backwards fast enough.

'For the last seven years, Anderson has been lying low, staying out of the limelight and out of trouble. But from what we saw and heard on the surveillance today, we now believe he's the frontman and salesman for a syndicate that is kidnapping and trafficking Australian women.' Erica glances around the room before continuing. 'And as the file in front of you indicates, he lives just one block from Heathcote train station. One block from where Ally Webster disappeared.

'We're still digging into his past, but we know Anderson did his time inside with the head of the Scorpions' money laundering operations: Nicholas Parelli, aka "Merlin".' Erica switches to an image of the bikie with a buzz cut and a greying goatee. The beard doesn't quite hide a narrow chin that makes him look like a bloated weasel. His eyes are cold, and a distinctive tattoo of a phoenix wraps around his neck.

'Today we got some great intel, solid leads that we've been lacking. But we still don't have any direct links between Anderson, Merlin and the missing women. We need more. We need proof Anderson is a part of this criminal operation. I'll be allocating assignments after this briefing. For now, any questions?'

Laura's task is to keep trawling the files for leads that may have been missed, but by the end of the day, all she has is eye strain and a burgeoning headache. She decides to walk it off, because Ki's also had a frustrating day in terms of exercise. They are no sooner home than she has him on the lead and out the door, and the cool night air immediately works to unwind her.

She's soon relaxed enough that her thoughts can disengage from the case, and drift instead to the one undeniably positive event of the day.

Once again, Leon had knocked softly at her door and talked her into a coffee run. Not that she needed much convincing. Leon is smart, funny and handsome in a geeky sort of way, plus he seems genuinely interested in her. Today's chat covered TV shows they're hooked on.

'I kind of like *Outlander*,' she'd said, unable to stop her face reddening with embarrassment – for her, the romance and time-travelling series is a guilty pleasure, and not something she would freely admit to, even to friends. Yet there she was, telling this guy she's only known for a few days.

How does he make me feel so at ease after such a short time?

'Aye, Sassenach,' Leon had replied, delivering the line with such bravado he could only be a fan himself, no matter that his Scottish accent was less-than-perfect.

Laura smiles at the memory. She'd almost snorted her coffee out of her nose, and even now, looking back, she's not sure if that was from amusement or surprise that Leon also watched the show. It's hardly blokey.

All of which, she realises, gives her a lot to think about. Since joining the force five years ago, she's had a few relationships but nothing long-lasting or serious. The guys she's dated have been fellow police officers, and after a passionate few months, the romances all fizzled out. After the first couple of times, she found she was hesitating to open up and be vulnerable; it was much easier to jettison the guys in question before things got too serious or intense, and before all the spark was gone.

Blushing, Leon had admitted to her that he already knew who she was before he met her. He confessed he'd been following her career from afar through the dog squad's social media pages and knew she and Ki had taken the title at the games.

When Laura laughed and asked if she should be worried about having a stalker, he reassured her it was all innocent but mumbled into his cup that he was enjoying getting to know the real Laura.

Smiling, she feels that this time it will be different. *Leon* feels different.

There's no point jumping too far ahead, but she's excited to see where this goes.

Chapter 8

Dan stares at the bottom of his glass, his eyes unfocused. He needs another drink, and he reaches for the almost empty bottle of Wild Turkey with hands the size of small plates. They shake as he slops out the amber liquid, spilling almost as much onto the coffee table as he pours into the glass.

He'll regret this binge in the morning but right now he needs to escape the noise in his head, the incessant buzzing in his ears that tells him he's made a mistake. But it's too late to back down. He has to trust Martin and her team to keep him safe. Keep him alive.

It had all fallen apart for him when he'd been caught selling drugs to an undercover officer at a gym. Before he would have taken the hit and done his time, but now he has Ellie to think of. Eight weeks ago, her mother – Dan's on-again-off-again lover – died of an overdose, and there was no way he could leave his daughter fatherless as well.

And so, he told police he was willing to cooperate and share information. He's already provided valuable insights into illegal drug operations at gyms across Sydney, but it was when he mentioned rumours that pretty, young Aussie women were being sourced for sale on the black market that his interviewers really sat up and took notice. From there, Leading Senior Constable Martin got involved. Now he's in so deep he can't picture a way out.

'Snitches get stitches,' he slurs into his drink, and laughs darkly.

Martin had been happy with the way he'd handled the meeting today but he knows tomorrow he has to seal the deal – get what the cops need to take down Cain Anderson and his syndicate. Then he can move on with his life. Move on with Ellie.

He grabs his phone, and it takes a few attempts before his clumsy fingers tap out the correct PIN. A photo of him cradling a newborn baby wrapped in a pink blanket appears onscreen. He loves this photo. Ellie looks like one of those kewpie dolls he used to hand to kids at the carnival, while he himself looks both stunned and proud at becoming a father.

He opens his photos folder and stares at a picture of Ellie taken three days ago. She's grown a lot in the last six months, despite suffering the withdrawals. Her mum had passed her drug addiction on to Ellie in the womb, and the process of recovery for his little girl has been hellish. While the worst is over, the doctors say she'll still have learning difficulties. To Dan, though, she is the most beautiful and precious thing in the world.

He wonders when he'll see her again. Hold her in his arms once more. Right now, his mum is in hiding with her, caring for her in safety while he tries to sort out the mess he's in.

His tears land on the screen, blurring the baby girl's face. His brothers at the club would say he's gone soft, but if he can get through the next few months, testify and move into witness protection, he'll have the money and means to support and protect Ellie for the rest of his life. So long as Martin upholds her end of the bargain.

And despite himself, he has started to trust the copper. She's a no-nonsense type and as straight as they come, but what worries him is the people she works with. The tentacles of organised crime reach deep into every part of society, and while he might be able to trust her, he has no idea who else knows that he is her source. Any one of them could leak that information back to people who'd have no hesitation about silencing him — permanently.

He decides the only way to deal with thoughts like that is to drown them and refills his glass. Soon, the room starts spinning, and he slides sideways onto the couch, his deep snores echoing through the empty house.

Chapter 9

Erica paces from the lounge to the kitchen and back, a continuous circuit of the cramped apartment they've been using as one of their safe houses.

Where is he?

Dan hasn't responded to her encrypted messages since last night. If he's getting cold feet, the whole operation falls apart.

Leon is playing a game on his tablet but Erica notices him glancing at her every now and again. Her tension is coming off her in waves.

An alarm sounds and Erica rushes to her phone, brings up the feed from the surveillance camera – Dan is strolling to the unit's front door.

There's the ping of the access code being accepted, then the door swings open and her informant staggers in. His eyes are bloodshot and a pungent whiskey aroma seeps from his pores.

Erica steps back from him, wrinkling her nose, 'Geez. Big night?' Dan looks at her, says nothing. 'Well, I hope you're up to this today.'

'I want this over,' he says. 'Just you remember the danger you're putting me in. You lot need to keep me and my kid safe.'

'I told you before, get us what we need and our deal is solid. Witness protection, a new identity, a new home, the works. Just don't get the shakes now. We're close.'

She searches out a large bottle of water and two aspirin, and watches as he swallows down the pills. When she's sure he's level, she hands him a bulging envelope of cash.

'Let's give the gear a last test,' she tells Leon, then leans in to address Dan. 'And you, run through it all again for me, just to make sure you've got it.

'What do you need to find out from Anderson?'

Just like last time, Dan knocks on the door of the small fibro cottage, mutters the password and is ushered inside. The only difference is that this time he's carrying a small gym bag.

'All teams, report in,' Erica says, her eyes never leaving the screen as her officers sound off. Everyone is in position, ready to rush the house.

She watches Cain lead the way to the lounge room; his body language betrays his irritation – the way he said nothing to Dan when he let him in, and strides ahead of him without looking back. Sure enough, he turns to face his guest, his hands on his hips. 'You're late. You were meant to be here by 10 am,' he snaps. 'I don't like to be kept waiting.'

'I had to do some dry cleaning,' Dan grunts.

'You what?'

Dan groans. 'I had to make sure no one was following me, didn't I?'

Cain leans in and sniffs. 'Yeah, right. You bloody stink of grog.'

'Whaddya care? Do you wanna do business or not?'

'Alright, princess, keep your shirt on. You got the twenty?'

Dan pulls the envelope from his bag and hands it over.

Cain fans the notes out, not bothering to count them, then gives Dan a slip of paper.

'This has all the info you need to get in. Once your buyers are in the online room they'll have up to 10 minutes to look at the girls. Trust me, that's generous for a payment this bloody small. If nothing tickles their fancy, you tell me what they're after. Sure I can rustle up something they'll like.'

'What if something does tickle their fancy?'

'There's going to be an auction, they can bid for the girls they want. Invitation only, entry fee in crypto. How much'll be confirmed in advance. They'll get a date and time and further instructions. If they make a purchase,' Anderson shrugs, 'well, they'll get a clean, young, top-shelf woman with a new look and new identity. Nothing to tie her to her old life.'

Erica listens, appalled. It takes all her self-control not to call in her team and drop this wicked man right there and then.

But an auction? That's more than she'd hoped for. Something like that, they could take down not only Cain but also the major players. Maybe even some of the syndicate's top brass. She's been working in the dark for so long, pulling at strings that unravel and go nowhere … this could save more than one woman's life.

Dan stuffs the paper into his pocket. 'All right, I'll pass this on and be in touch.'

'Don't take too long,' Cain warns. 'They won't want to miss out because you stopped off to pick up your dry cleaning.'

'Good job,' Erica says as Dan collapses onto the couch at the safe house and Leon busies himself removing the listening and video devices from him. 'We got some excellent intel today.'

'Well, that's great,' he replies. 'So, we're done now, right? I'm finished?'

'Not quite. We need your help just a little longer.'

Dan leaps to his feet, causing Leon to stumble backwards and almost crash into the coffee table. 'That wasn't part of our deal!' he yells, jabbing his finger at Erica's face. 'You said all I had to do was get you access to the women! Prove Anderson is the frontman and you'd take it from there! You got any idea the tightrope I'm walking here? Or don't you care?'

Erica steps in so the two are almost eye to eye, her nostrils flaring as she stares the big man down. She wants to tell him to stop being a dick and pull his head in, but that'll just trigger him to walk, and she needs him.

'Yes, I understand. Of course, I do. But we have an opening with this auction. It's a chance to take the group down. We can't pass that up.'

'Find someone else!' Dan rages, spittle flying from his mouth. Erica holds her breath against the foul stench of whiskey. 'I've done what you wanted, now keep your end of the bargain!'

'Your ongoing cooperation will help your case for witness protection –'

'What do you mean, *help my case*? You said we were solid! You telling me it's not legit? You been playing me this whole time?'

Leon has positioned himself on the couch now and shrinks into the cushions as Dan seems to swell, the louder his voice gets.

Erica remains still, unflinching. Her eyes narrow as she focuses on her breathing, to squash her rising anger. 'No,' she says. 'Calm down.' She enunciates each word with slow deliberation. 'There *is* a deal. What I *am* saying is that it could get better. Lifetime support for your daughter. We know she has special needs. Protection for your mother, too. You'll never have to worry about money or your daughter's future again.'

For a moment, it looks like he will lunge forward and wring her neck. Instead, Dan steps back, rubs his bloodshot eyes and sits back down. 'All right. What's next?'

Chapter 10

Edging the curtains back, Cain Anderson watches Tiny amble off the porch and down the street, then turns his attention to counting the cash. The twenty is there, but something still feels off to him.

He'd expected the big fella to try to negotiate more screen time for his money; instead, he just took what was offered, like some kind of amateur. And thinking about it, sure, he's got the Scorpions tatt, but he's never mentioned anything about the higher-ups – the President, Sergeant-at-Arms or any of the top dogs – wanting to get involved in the deal.

Cain goes back and forth in his head. Should he call Merlin? Check this guy Tiny out properly?

But he's reluctant to call his old cellmate from Goulburn Gaol. Once upon a time Merlin was a certified accountant, but now he coordinates global money laundering operations for the Scorpions. He earned his nickname for his magical ability to make money disappear.

He's also one of the best hustlers Cain's ever met. If he sniffs an opportunity, he'll take it. And if Cain asks about Tiny, he'll have to talk about the girls and the auction and the rest of the set up, and then Merlin will demand to get in on the action.

Then, of course, he'd have to explain to his boss that the main moneyman for the Scorpions knows about their venture and wants a cut. Plus, his boss will crucify him anyway if he's taken on a buyer who's cooked.

But he can't shake the feeling Tiny's hiding something.

Running his fingers through his unruly grey hair, Cain pulls a phone from his pocket and makes the call.

By midday, Cain's already sitting at a corner table with a glass of red in a private back room that also doubles as storage for the Star Tavern – a space reserved for VIP customers. When his contact appears, he's carrying a beer and weaves past stacked boxes and crates of alcohol. It's been a while since Cain has seen him, but the greying goatee, buzz cut, and elaborate neck tattoo that peeks out from beneath the brown t-shirt and leather jacket are just as he remembers.

Merlin squeezes his bulging stomach behind the table opposite Cain, shakes hands and takes off his sunglasses. 'Long time, no see,' he says. 'What's up? You sounded worried.'

As with any industry, time is money in the criminal world, and Cain dives right in. 'I've started doing business with a big fella by the name of Tiny. He has the club tatt and makes out he's working for the Scorpions, but something's off about him.' Cain sips from his wine and then winces. 'Jesus. I don't know why I thought I'd get a decent merlot in this dive.'

'Why did you switch to that crap? Should've stuck to beer.'

'Too gassy. Bloats me up like a dead fish.'

'Too much information, mate,' Merlin jokes. He cracks his knuckles and tilts his head toward his old cellmate. 'All right, so first, I need to make sure this bloke is who he says he is. Tell me everything you can about him and why he's talking to you.'

'Big unit. Likes his gym gear. Lots of tatts, as well as the club one. Wears a baseball cap all the time.'

'And what's the business he's sticking his beak into?'

'Trafficking on the dark web.'

'Trafficking what?'

'Women.'

Merlin strokes his goatee, looks like he's waiting for more, but Cain stops short of giving away anything that indicates who he's working for. 'All right,' he says at last. 'Let me make a coupla calls.'

He moves away from the table and pulls out his phone. After a minute or two, he hangs up.

'Want another?' he asks, indicating Cain's drink. Then he pauses to check a small screen on the wall that provides a view of the corridor outside and pulls open a hidden door to the bar.

When he returns to the table, it's with two schooners. He pushes one to Cain. 'Try this, it's a lot better than that swill.' He swigs from his own glass and sits back. 'Okay. So, the man you described is Tiny, and he is one of ours. He's not old school, more of a Nike Bikie, but he's been useful. He's got solid connections to gyms across the city, he knows and is trusted by the buyers, and he runs deliveries. He's been reliable and helped us expand, but nobody's heard from him in months. He had a kid, then his missus OD'd. Baby's got some medical problems, so the club's left him alone to get his shit together.' He takes another drink. 'Thing is, no one knew he was getting into this. He's definitely not repping us; might be trading on our name for a side hustle.'

'What does that mean?'

'It means,' Merlin says as he throws back the last of his beer and wipes his mouth with the back of his hand. He eyes Cain's untouched glass, then pulls it towards him, 'I'll dig into this with some close friends. When I know more, I'll be in touch.'

'What do you want me to do in the meantime? He could be working with the pigs. I might be exposed.'

'You want my advice?' Merlin asks and Cain nods. 'Play along for now. But be cautious. Don't give him as much as you said you would. See what he does and how he reacts. I'll get back to you soon, and if we find he's gone over, we'll deal with it. And you … you'll owe me.'

'What do you mean?'

'We're scratching your back; you'll need to scratch ours. We want a cut of the profit.'

Cain pushes back from the table and, in his rush, knocks over his wine. The glass shatters on the dirty concrete floor, the drink spreading like a bloodstain at his feet. 'I can't okay that.'

Merlin rises from his seat and places his arm around his old cellmate's shoulders. 'Well, brother, we can always leave Tiny alone. Let him chat to the cops and see how that works out for you? Whaddya say?'

Cain slips out of Merlin's grip, eyes cast to the ground. 'I'll make some calls.'

'You do that,' Merlin replies.

Chapter 11

As Cain Anderson left the weatherboard house in Heathcote and hopped in a taxi, Leon was already on the phone to Erica to tell her the suspect was on the move.

She's had Leon monitoring Anderson from hidden cameras around his property ever since Cain's first meeting with Dan and immediately orders two of her officers to shadow him. They tail him to the Star Tavern, parking a short distance away as he gets out of his cab and enters the establishment.

In a few short minutes, Leon has joined the officers in their car and fits Kyle, the younger of the two men, with monitoring devices while talking him through how to enable a small listening and recording device as well as a camera in a tattered baseball cap. Dressed in old jeans, boots and a faded black AC/DC t-shirt, Kyle pushes a small, flesh-coloured ball into his ear before jamming the hat over his shoulder-length, straggly mullet.

'Are we on?' he asks as he strides through the car park.

'Loud and clear,' Leon replies from back in the van. 'We're getting good visual and audio.'

Erica's voice crackles in the officer's ear. 'Take it easy. Don't engage Anderson. Order a beer, place a bet, just hang out. I want to find out what he's up to without spooking him.'

As the door swings open, the murmur of voices and noise of a race call on a TV comes over the top of the live feed. The pub is dark and dingy, chipped bar tables and cheap stools complete the depressing picture. Erica can imagine Kyle's feet sticking to the worn carpet with each step across a surface left tacky by decades of spilt drinks. He peers around the room, the camera in his cap relaying the view of three tradies by the window enjoying parmies and pints, and an older man who sways in his stool as he tries to follow the horse racing on a telly in the corner.

It takes a moment before Erica realises there's no sign of Anderson.

'Did he slip out the back?' she asks.

'Negative,' replies the second surveillance officer, who's watching the rear exit.

'So, he's there somewhere,' Erica murmurs. 'Sit tight.'

The low rumble of a motorcycle engine grows louder before cutting out, and a moment later a bearded man in a leather jacket, dark sunglasses and neck tattoo thrusts open the front door, calling out to the barman and ordering a schooner of beer before he's even fully inside the room. He chats with the surly-looking publican while he fills the glass, then takes his drink and struts towards a door with a sign pointing to the restrooms.

'Time for a break,' Erica orders and Kyle downs his beer before also heading down the hallway. The feed from his camera shows him glancing left and right as he looks for the bikie. He pushes open the door to the men's and checks the room. All the cubicles are empty and no one's at the urinal.

Returning to the corridor he looks for another doorway or exit, but the video shows nothing.

'He's not here,' he whispers.

'What the hell?' Erica replies. 'He can't just disappear. Check the women's as well.'

Erica watches as Kyle's hand reaches out to push open the door to the female toilet. He freezes when a voice speaks from behind him.

'You lost, mate? You don't look like a sheila to me.' The barman stands in the corridor, gesturing to the male restroom. 'You'll be wanting that one.'

'Thanks, that could've been embarrassing,' Kyle says, covering quickly. 'My missus keeps telling me I need glasses and should get my eyes checked but I haven't wanted to believe her. Looks like she's right. Again,' he jokes, and Erica watches as the barman says nothing, his face expressionless as he stands with his hands on his hips, making sure his patron gets the right door this time.

Kyle goes to a cubicle, closes the door behind him and waits for a minute or two before flushing, washing his hands and returning to the bar. The bartender nods to him then resumes his task of wiping glasses.

'Can I get another beer, mate?'

The gruff barkeep pulls a schooner, and as he does so, the bikie with the goatee walks back in from the restroom corridor. He holds up two fingers, and the bartender gives him the thumbs up.

Kyle drags an abandoned newspaper towards him on the bar and pulls out the form guide. He makes a show of checking the odds on the TV screen – Erica notes the next race is at Randwick.

The bikie slides over to him as he waits for his drinks.

'Like a flutter do you, mate?' His voice is raspy, like someone who's smoked all their life, or taken one too many hits to the throat.

'Now and then. You got a tip for the next one?'

'No idea. Don't follow the ponies myself. Never had an interest in it. You're better off playing the market. More chance of getting at least some of your dough back. Just got to be patient. Ride out the lows and wait for the highs.'

Grasping the fresh beers, he whispers, 'Get into crypto, that's my advice.' Then he's away again through the door to the restrooms.

'Stay there,' Erica instructs. 'Place a bet and watch the races. If you follow him again, it'll seem suss, and I don't like the look of the barman. Too curious for my liking.'

Kyle places wagers on the next two races and exclaims loudly when his pick in the first is pipped at the post. The jockeys are easing jittery thoroughbreds into stalls for the next race when Cain Anderson emerges from the hallway, nodding to the barman before leaving the pub. From the van outside, Erica watches him hail a taxi and drive away.

Back inside, the bikie reappears. Leaning over the bar, he chats to the publican before approaching the undercover officer.

'Do any good?'

'Got second. Waiting for the next race now. I've gone for a roughie. Figured the payout would be worth it.'

'Ha. Good luck to you,' the bikie says, then heads outside.

'We have eyes on him,' Erica says to Kyle. 'Stay there until the race is run, collect your winnings and head to the car.'

Chapter 12

Laura and Ki enter the briefing room, summoned on the double by their taskforce leader, like everyone else on the team. There's a buzz among the group about what could be that urgent, and everyone is looking at the newcomer standing by Erica at the main screen as the source of answers. She's tall, her short black hair streaked with blue highlights, and wears jeans, a white t-shirt and a grey tailored jacket, with Converse sneakers. But it's the hot-pink, manicured nails she sports that draw Laura's eyes.

'Thanks for coming so quickly, everyone,' Erica begins. 'There's been some developments with Cain Anderson but we're going to have to wait on those for a while because CIU have something for us that's happening right now. We have a live feed to their ops room. Bec, are you ready?'

The name shakes something loose in Laura's head, and she realises the woman must be Dr Bec Walraven, the formidable head of the Cyber Intelligence Unit. Handpicked by the NSW Police while still at university, she has a PhD and is one of the leading experts on hacking and the dark web. At just 27, she leads a team of young guns who work from a high-security, restricted room that everyone in headquarters calls the Shark Cage.

She nods at Erica before slipping on a headset and saying, 'Let's roll.'

Prompts to enter passwords appear on the screen, and Laura watches as someone back at the Shark Cage keys them in. The website's tiny progress wheel turns agonisingly slowly, then the display switches to an online waiting room.

The shadowy outline of a woman appears. A strobe light starts up, its flashes giving them brief glimpses of her bound, gagged and lying on a four-poster bed. She's wearing lacy, almost see-through red underwear, and a bright blue wig hides her true hair colour. An intricate, black-feathered mask covers the upper half of her face. She's sluggish, her movements slow. Either she's frightened to death or heavily sedated. Or both.

The screen goes dark and the wheel turns again before a different woman appears. The flashing lights make it difficult to get a good look at her, but she's kneeling on a bed and decked out in black leather. Her face is fully covered by a mask depicting a deer head, and she jerks in response to a whip that is flicked across her bottom.

Everything goes black once more before a new image comes into focus. This time, a petite woman is lying on a chaise longue. She's dressed in a skimpy schoolgirl outfit, feathered gold mask and long blonde wig tied into pig tails. Almost immediately, the image of her disappears.

The team watch and wait for more. Thirty seconds go by, but it feels like an eternity.

'What's going on?' Bec demands. 'We had less than five minutes.' She listens to her headset for a moment, then says, 'Keep trying to get back in.'

'What's happening?' Erica asks.

'I don't know. It could be a glitch. We thought we'd get more time.' Bec toggles the mike on her headset. 'Give me good news.'

A pause, then Bec shakes her head. 'It's no good. We're locked out.'

'What does that mean?' Erica asks, her voice sharp. 'Do you think they suspect something? Can you tell where they were streaming from?'

'I don't know. They could be suspicious, and that's why we got less time than we thought we would and were booted out. Or it could be a system error, or even a ploy to squeeze more money for extra screen time. I'm not sure. Whatever it is, we could only use the passwords once, so now we're out, we can't get back in. And no, we can't tell where they were broadcasting from. They hid it well.'

Erica turns to Leon. 'I want you to work with Bec's crew on this. Try enhancing those images. Look for defining physical characteristics, anything that might tell us who these women are. Call me as soon as you have something.'

She turns to face the rest of the team. 'Meanwhile, I want constant updates on Cain Anderson. We trailed him to a meeting with Merlin earlier today, but we need to keep tabs on where he is and what he's doing.'

As the team rush off, Laura watches as Erica opens her laptop and taps out a frantic text message.

Someone's in trouble …

Chapter 13

Leon gathers his crew – Jess, fresh out of university and eager to prove herself, and Matt, a career-changer in his early thirties. Until last year, Matt was an electrician but is now completing an IT degree while working for the NSW Police as a contractor. He'd set his sights on a job with Bec Walraven's team, but with no spots available, he took a post with the main taskforce instead.

Allocating them both footage and screenshots of each woman provided by Bec, Leon joins them to sift through the material. Comparing the images from the website with their own file pictures of the missing women, they start looking for any physical features to indicate that any of the three women they viewed may be one of the five they are searching for.

Leon takes the footage of the second woman, whose face and neck had been covered by the deer-head mask. He plays, pauses and replays the video of her over and over until his eyes are sore, but finally he thinks he has something.

Winding back the footage he's looked at so many times already, he freezes it at a moment when the woman flinches from the whip. The motion lifts the mask from her shoulders for a millisecond, just enough to pick up ...

Heart racing, he turns to his second monitor, scanning the file photos before enlarging the one of Siobhan Kennedy.

There it is. A mole on the side of her neck, small but visible.

Returning to the website images, he enlarges and enhances the image, but it just gets grainier and fuzzier.

'Matt. Jess. Come and have a look at this.' Stopping work, his colleagues crowd around his screens. 'What do you think it is?'

'Could be a mole,' Jess concedes, comparing the two images.

'Could be a mark from the mask resting on her neck, too. It looks heavy,' Matt says.

Frustrated, Leon slumps back in his seat. 'How are you two going?'

'Not sure,' Jess offers; she's been examining the footage of the first woman. 'No tattoos, recognisable moles, birthmarks or other defining physical characteristics. Maybe one thing, though.'

'Go on,' Leon says, pulling his chair next to hers.

'Well, she's wearing that mask, and her eyes are mostly closed, but there's a moment here –' Jess pauses her footage and enlarges it '– just there. Blue eyes and those might be faint freckles on her cheek.'

Leon assesses the screen. Based on that, the woman could be Tori Engel, but the poor light and limited screen time make it almost impossible to tell.

'Take some screenshots,' he says, 'then take a break. Refresh your eyes. And how about you, Matt? Found anything yet?'

'Not really,' Matt answers from his desk. 'I've cross-checked the footage and photos. The mask is heavily feathered and shields her eyes. It's more like a blindfold, so I can't get a clear view. She has a small build and that fits with Sophie Romano. She's only 155 cm tall and very slim but that's it. Nothing concrete.'

'Keep at it for a bit longer, then we'll regroup. I'll make a coffee run.'

As he sits on a bench, waiting for the brews, Leon can't help but think of Laura. Coffee runs had become their thing now, but in the last day, things had progressed. Knowing she was an *Outlander* fan, he'd taken the chance on booking two tickets for a new film with the show's star, Sam Heughan. He'd hesitated before telling her but finally screwed up his courage and asked her if she'd like to go with him.

Words can't describe his feelings when she'd said yes.

He's not sure what it is about her that's got to him this way. In team meetings, she comes across as serious and even distant, but when they're together and she smiles … He loves her red hair, the freckles on her nose and cheeks, and her blue, blue eyes. And it's impossible for him to act cool around her; he feels like a dithering fool whenever they chat.

But she still spends time with him.

Right now, it's all he needs to get through days like this.

He's humming under his breath as he returns to the team, laden with fresh coffees, wraps and sandwiches. Little treats to perk the team up, the way the thought of Laura has lifted him. He hands Jess her cup and turns to drop off Matt's before noticing the empty workstation.

'Where's he gone?' he asks.

'Said he needed a break for some fresh air,' Jess replies. 'Told me to tell you he won't be long.'

Dropping the coffee and food on Matt's desk, Leon returns to his screens and focuses on enhancing what might be Siobhan Kennedy's mole. When Matt does return, he barely even notices.

That evening, at the movie, Leon buys popcorn and is thrilled as Laura leans into him to share it. It builds his confidence enough to try and take her hand, and when she doesn't pull away, all thoughts of his physically and emotionally draining day vanish.

After the film, they grab a drink and talk, the conversation flowing like they're old friends, and continuing in the car on the way to drop her home.

'So, you never said,' Laura begins, 'how long you've been with the team.'

'Five years with Tech, well before the taskforce was formed,' he replies. 'But this is my first time as a team leader.'

'You like it? Being in charge?'

'I like being a mentor,' he answers. 'And I love the work. But maybe not the hours. So how about you – why dogs?'

Laura laughs. 'To be honest, I never even wanted to be a police officer. I always wanted to be a vet or a farmer. COVID messed that up,' she pauses a second. 'And some other things going on in my life meant I didn't get the marks for veterinary science. But I'd met Erica while I was in high school, we became friends, and I admired her dedication and drive. So here I am, following her example.'

'Dogs,' Leon prompts with a smile.

She laughs. 'Just because I couldn't be a vet, didn't mean I stopped wanting to work with animals.'

They pull in outside her house and he turns off the engine. The weight of the moment hangs heavy between them.

'Well, it's late,' Laura says. 'And we both have work in the morning, so …'

Leon leans in, and she responds by running her fingers over his beard.

Emboldened, he grasps her hand in his, and his heart soars as their lips meet.

Chapter 14

The diagram that dominates the screen looks like an intricate spider's web. At the centre are the faces of the five missing women. From them, lines stretch and criss-cross, touching on Cain Anderson, and connecting Anderson to Merlin and to the silhouette of a face that represents Erica's informant, Dan.

Anderson's meeting with the influential Scorpion was a breakthrough. Long gone are the days when criminal groups and bikie gangs ran closed shops; Erica knows modern criminal networks are fluid, willing to collaborate and work with each other for the right opportunity, with arrangements that can reach well beyond Australia's borders. The previous relationship between cellmates Anderson and Merlin could be the foundation of one such criminal partnership.

If only they'd had eyes and ears on the pair's meeting. Erica would love to know what they discussed.

Frustrated, Erica returns her attention to the screen, but there's no relief there – the image still shows more question marks than faces. She presses a hand to her forehead and sighs. She has a briefing with Assistant Commissioner Stirling and the DC this afternoon, and despite the breakthrough with Anderson and

Merlin, this won't be enough to satisfy them. She brings up the screenshots and video clips from Leon and his team. The images are inconclusive, the evidence nowhere near definitive, but Erica circles Siobhan's and Tori's faces on the map.

She needs to keep Dan calm and onside. He's her one solid link to Anderson, and the key to securing a place at the auction.

There's a knock on the door. She looks up to find Laura waiting and waves her in.

'I finished doing a first full review of Detective Ryan's files,' Laura starts as she pulls the door closed behind her.

'I need some good news. Tell me you found something.'

'I'm not sure,' Laura replies, biting on her lower lip.

'Then tell me what you think you know and we'll go from there.'

'Okay,' Laura says, and Erica motions for her to take a seat. 'Ryan couldn't find any connection between the women: they're not related, have different career paths, and have none of the same friends, interests or hobbies. But what Ryan didn't know – that we do – is Cain Anderson's possible role in all of this. We know Anderson is connected to the Scorpions, so I looked more closely at the locations where the women disappeared, using that information as a filter. I mapped each place against known chapters of the gang, and it's a mixed bag. As expected, they have strong membership and reach in Sydney and Newcastle, but there's no record of any significant activity in Leeton or

Armidale. That doesn't mean they don't have influence in those places, but there's no current, confirmed active presence.

'So, I started examining other criminal activity in the two regions. Leeton is less than an hour's drive from Griffith, which is well known for its past connections to the 'Ndrangheta.'

Erica nods. She'd considered the involvement of the Australian mafia – most famous for the disappearance and suspected murder of anti-drug campaigner Donald Mackay in 1977 – as possible players in any people trafficking operations, but nothing had yet pointed to them.

'From my brief discussion with the Superintendent in charge of the Murrumbidgee District, the 'Ndrangheta are still active but are more covert and harder to detect now. They're cleverer at concealing themselves than they were in the days of Trimboli and Mackay and have some influential political connections. He told me they're also monitoring a growing, local chapter of the Bandidos. Armidale's farming and university communities are close to areas where there is a strong, ongoing demand for illegal drugs. I haven't talked to the local police yet but there've been recent arrests for cannabis and meth production out that way, with suspected ties to Asian crime gangs and the Aussie mafia. In Sydney and Newcastle, the 'Ndrangheta has always been a player.'

Erica pulls her gaze from Laura back to the web of intersecting lines and faces on her screen, her eyes drawn to Cain Anderson. 'Anything else?'

'I did notice Detective Ryan had pulled Ally Webster's file and added it to his case notes. He may have picked up a clue that linked her to these latest cases but I haven't been able to work it out. Not yet.'

'Interesting,' Erica says. 'I didn't know he'd started investigating Ally. Keep on it. Search for any connection between Anderson and the other criminal groups. I'll chase Assistant Commissioner Stirling, find out when we're getting someone to replace Ryan.'

'One more thing,' Erica says as Laura gets up to leave. 'I'd like you and Ki to go to Griffith, check in with Superintendent Hewson and chat to him and his team – in person. Try to arrange a visit to the winery at Leeton where Sophie Romano performed. Let's investigate further if the places where our missing women worked have any serious criminal links.'

Alone again, Erica returns her attention to the monitor, her finger circling Anderson's face.

'Who are you working for?' she whispers.

Chapter 15

Thorny roses weave and spread like tentacles covering the old farmhouse, blocking her access. Laura pants as she struggles to break through, wincing as sharp edges tear at her clothes and slash at her skin. Brilliant-red blood splashes on the cracked and worn path, and the woody branches part before her as if tribute has now been paid.

She falls onto the front step and pushes the door open, clutching at her arms and legs to stem the bleeding.

'Laura, is that you? You're just in time for lunch.'

That voice. So familiar. So loved.

Laura crawls forward, her blood leaving a vivid trail, like a macabre Hansel and Gretel, and finds her Gran – Grace Murray – seated at the head of the large family table. Her face is round and her hair shiny, like it was before the cancer left her looking like a broken, fragile bird. Her favourite Blue Flow porcelain pot and teacup are in front of her, and she glances up from them as her granddaughter drags herself into the kitchen.

'Laura,' she gasps. 'What on earth happened to you?'

'I had a fall.'

Rushing from her seat, she pulls out a chair for Laura before fetching antiseptic and bandages. As her wounds are cleaned, Laura reaches out and touches her grandmother's face. 'I've missed you, Gran.'

'That's lovely, but you need to be more careful,' Grace replies as she swipes a solution onto Laura's torn skin that stings and burns. 'I won't always be around to keep an eye on you or patch you up.'

'I know,' Laura whispers, ignoring the pain in her body and the ache in her heart.

Her grandmother pats her on the arm and pours her a steaming cup of Irish Breakfast. 'Have some tea, it'll help.'

Laura does as she's told. She'd do anything to keep Gran with her.

As she drains the last of the brew, Gran holds out her hand. 'Pass it over. It's time I did a reading for you, don't you think?' She winks and pulls the delicate china towards her.

Grace lifts the cup to her face, turning it one way and then the other, gazing at its contents. 'Ooh, Laura, there's someone special in your life. There's a young man you fancy, isn't there?' Laura nods. 'He's quite handsome. He looks after his family. He seems like a good boy but ...'

'What? But what?' Laura's heart races. She's desperate for reassurance her romantic interest in Leon is not a mistake.

'There's someone else. He's …' Gran's words falter. Her body twists and rocks in the chair, convulsing so hard her head snaps back and forth before she slumps lifeless on the table.

'No! Gran! Gran! Wake up!' Laura rushes to Grace's side and feels for a pulse. There's none. 'I needed more time!' she sobs. 'I didn't tell you I love you!'

'What about me? Do you love me, sweet thing?'

Gary emerges from the darkness of the hallway into the bright, sunlit kitchen.

'Get out!' Laura shouts at him as she hovers protectively over her grandmother. 'You're not welcome!'

'The old duck carked it, hey!' Gary smirks. 'We all have to go sometime, right? And death's not that bad, not when you get to return and visit those you care about.' He edges closer. 'Granny thinks your new bloke is a good guy. How romantic. But what do you *really* know about him? I don't think he's worthy. He's not as devoted as I am.' His face is so close to Laura now that she can feel his breath on her skin.

'You know nothing about devotion or love!' Laura shouts as she pushes him in the chest. 'Get out!'

'All right, all right,' Gary says, holding his hands up in placation. 'You think I don't know about love? Maybe. But I do know about revenge.' Chuckling, he fades into the shadows. 'Till next time, sweetie!'

A low whine wakes her from her dream – Ki is crying in his crate in her room. Laura shakes the sleep from her head, as if trying to purge the vision, drags herself out of bed, and then releases her best friend. Ki clambers onto her lap, licking her face and she buries her head in his fur, soaking him with tears.

Chapter 16

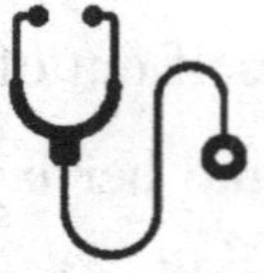

Meg Harrison's eyes in the Missing Persons poster on the staff room wall seem to follow Simon as he slots a second pod into the coffee machine and inhales the aroma of the double-shot espresso dripping down into his cup. Two nurses are chatting in a corner, and he waves at them before taking his coffee and his phone and sinking into a comfy armchair.

At 33, Simon is old for an intern, but he didn't have the same sheltered and loving upbringing as many of his colleagues. An abusive father, a mother who left with Simon when he was two to get away from that abuse. Then, after she died in a car accident when he was 13, he was taken in by his only remaining relative – his uncle, a confirmed bachelor who struggled with becoming an instant parent. Six years ago, his uncle passed away from cancer, a nightmarish experience that compelled Simon to become a doctor. He had to pass additional courses and testing to meet the prerequisites for medicine, all the while supporting himself through his studies.

Every step of his journey has been a struggle, and now that he's in his final year of training, he's determined to make the most of any opportunities. Moving from nearby Liverpool to the bigger Parramatta District Hospital was one of them.

'You're welcome to join us, doctor,' the older of the two women calls, and he breathes deeply before smiling, stowing his phone and heading over to the nurses' table.

'How are you finding it here?' the younger nurse asks as he pulls out a chair. He guesses she's in her mid-twenties, a cute brunette with large, doe-like brown eyes and a cheeky, friendly vibe. Her accent betrays British heritage, and Simon can tell straight off that she connects well with people and must be popular with patients.

'It's very welcoming,' he replies as he blows on his steaming beverage. 'Very professional.'

'How long will you be with us in A&E, doctor?' the older woman asks. Now he looks at her properly, he recognises her as one of the supervising sisters.

'Two months, then I move to paediatrics, surgery and the geriatric ward. But I'm hoping to swap one of my rotations for a stint with obstetrics.' He rubs his eyes; they're hot and gritty with fatigue. He really needs the coffee to start working.

'It's designed to test you,' the sister says, touching his arm. 'You know that, don't you? The double shifts, the constant questioning by the registrars and senior doctors. Just take it one day at a time, you'll be all right.' She checks the time on a fob watch pinned to the front of her scrubs, and exhales deeply before easing herself out of the chair. 'Back to the craziness,' she says, and rolls her eyes. 'There's nothing quite like A&E on a full moon.'

'She's right, you know,' the younger nurse says as her colleague heads out. 'They really hammer the new doctors. It's worse in the UK; they deliberately try to break you there, to test if you have what it takes.'

'Where did you work?' Simon asks. He sips from his mug again, desperate for the caffeine to kick in. 'London?'

'I trained at Royal London, mainly in Emergency.'

'What made you move here?'

'COVID,' she replies. 'Dealing with the heartbroken families who couldn't be with their loved ones at the end. I couldn't take it anymore, so I quit. I had an Aussie boyfriend, who'd already returned home, so I decided to follow him.'

'I'm sensing that didn't go how you planned.'

She laughs, half amused, half bitter. 'When I got here, turns out he had another girl. Or two. Or three. So, I was stuck on the other side of the world with no partner, no money and no job. I wasn't about to go home with my tail between my legs, so here I am.' She raises her hands in the air, gesturing at the scene around her. 'Wow. Sorry. I didn't mean to dump that on you. We've only just met.'

'That's all right,' Simon says. He smiles, knowing that shows off his dimples to good effect. 'Sometimes it helps to talk to a stranger. And for the record, he sounds like an idiot. I'm sure you can do better.' He holds out his hand. 'I'm Simon. Simon Russell.'

'Eve Crawley,' she replies as they shake. She checks her watch, and the moment passes. 'I'd better get going. Sister will be on my back if I'm late, and like she said, full moon tonight. All the nutters will be out in force!'

Simon watches as she closes the break room door behind her, then pulls his phone out of his pocket. He sits in silence, drinking his coffee as he reads his messages. There's a text from Erica:

WORKING LATE. MISS YOU. WAKE ME UP WHEN YOU GET HOME 😊.

Simon takes a photo of his empty coffee cup and attaches it to his reply.

BREAK OVER. BACK TO WORK! SEE YOU SOON, MY LOVE.

He places his dirty mug in the dishwasher and heads back to his rounds. Silently, from her place on the wall, Meg Harrison watches him go.

Chapter 17

Erica wakes to find Simon is spooning her, his long legs curled behind hers, arm draped over her as he sleeps. His snores are soft and mellow. She must've gotten too warm in the night, with his body wrapped around hers, because she's pushed the doona back so it's only covering her from the hips down.

Simon had done as she'd asked and woken her when he got home. They'd made love, slow and tender at first and then with increasing intensity, clinging to each other in their climax. She'd like nothing more than to stay in bed and repay the favour by waking him up for round two, but she has a busy day ahead and wants to squeeze in a run before she leaves. The taskforce has been so consuming, she's neglected her own health and fitness.

Unfolding herself from her lover, she swings her legs out of bed before dragging the doona up around Simon again and kissing him lightly on the forehead. He stirs and murmurs something that sounds like 'BP is dropping', then rolls over and resumes snoring.

Moving quietly so she doesn't wake him, Erica pulls on running gear and sneakers, grabs her keys and phone, then steps onto the front porch. The streetlamps are still on, but pink streaks of light poke between the houses and apartment buildings, and the traffic is already building up as she starts a slow jog up the road.

Simon is still asleep when she returns, and she silently strips off for a shower. The hot water stings her cold, sweaty skin and she lingers under the spray before washing herself clean. She's out and drying off before she realises a naked Simon is standing in the doorway, watching her.

'Enjoying the show?' she laughs.

'Sure am.' He steps into the tiny ensuite and drags her toward him. 'Fancy getting all dirty again?' he murmurs as his tongue works its way up her neck to her lips.

'So much,' she answers, 'but I need to get a wriggle on. Not a good look for the boss to be late.'

'Are you sure?' Simon asks and slides his hands down her lower back to her bottom.

Erica traps his hands and pulls them away. 'I'm sure. Anyway, don't you have to get ready too?'

'Yes,' Simon sighs, and turns on the shower again.

'Then I'll get the coffee going.'

Simon's singing echoes in the bathroom as she grinds the beans. Before he came into her life, she was a boring Nescafé girl; now he's turned her into a coffee snob, and she'll only suffer instant if there's nothing else available. In return, she's got him drinking herbal tea, a major achievement for someone who essentially runs on caffeine and adrenaline.

She's partway through a bowl of muesli and yoghurt when Simon saunters into the kitchen in freshly pressed black scrubs. He runs his fingers down her shoulder, then takes his coffee and sits beside her at the island bench. 'Do you think you'll be late tonight?' he asks.

'We're getting to a critical point, so probably. I'll let you know later. What about you?'

'I'm only rostered on for the afternoon shift, but who knows, things can change. Last night was insane. One guy came in, and you won't believe what he'd stuffed –'

'I don't want to know!'

'I mean it was jammed in there so hard, he needed surgery.'

Erica almost spits out her coffee laughing. 'Stop it!'

Simon grins and pours himself some muesli too. 'So, you're getting close to a breakthrough, hey? Got the crooks right where you want them?'

'Wouldn't say that. But I've got a good team and our best lead so far.' She doesn't elaborate. Simon knows better than to ask for details she's duty-bound not to reveal.

'Maybe when the taskforce is done and I finish my rotations we can get away for a short holiday? Maybe the Whitsundays. Or even Bali?'

Erica stoops to kiss him. 'That sounds wonderful. Have a good day. Fingers crossed no one's pushed anything into any weird places today.'

Simon pulls her closer, and as his tongue finds hers, desire rushes through her.

'God, I love a woman in uniform,' he mutters and releases her from the clinch. 'Go get 'em, officer.'

Erica parks in her assigned spot in the basement and heads quickly up to her office. The daily briefing is in an hour, and she has to prep for it.

She's almost done and is reviewing her case files and notes one last time when the phone rings.

'Erica? Assistant Commissioner Stirling,' the voice announces when she picks up.

'Good morning, sir.'

'I know you're due in a briefing, so I'll make this quick. Just wanted to let you know we've sourced a new detective to help examine those criminal networks and businesses you're looking into. Should be with you by the end of the day. Name of Alexandra Jeffries, you may have heard of her?'

'Thank you, sir, and yes, I have. Detective Jeffries has an impressive track record for results. She'll be a welcome asset to the team. I'll have someone waiting to get her up to speed.'

'Very good. I won't keep you then.'

'Thank you again, sir. We'll put her to good use.'

Erica hangs up and grabs her gear to head to the briefing room, only to find her way blocked by Bec Walraven, who's appeared in the door. Today, the head of the cyber unit's nails are a pale mint, and she's wearing a long denim skirt, cowgirl boots and a loose, matching green shirt. It's a far cry from the power suits and killer heels that define many women in positions of authority and she admires Bec for being her own person.

'Do you have a moment?' Bec asks, then closes the door behind her and sinks into a chair without waiting for an answer. 'I think I'm onto something that may help your investigation.'

Erica puts down the files for the briefing and returns to her seat. 'Go on.'

'It's early days,' Bec begins, twirling a pen between her fingers, 'but something came up in a job I'm doing for another operation. We had a tip-off a little while ago about a new encrypted app. Seems it's fast becoming the go-to platform for criminal groups in Australia as we've heard it mentioned in several taped conversations between different networks. They call it *TITAN*. I haven't worked out if that stands for anything or if it's just a name, but it's being plugged as a safe and secure platform for multi-criminal group communication.'

'Can you access it?' Erica asks.

'We're working on it, but at least now we know it's out there. Once we get in, we should find out who's playing in the sandpit, including whether your main lead and suspect is using it.'

'Was that website link our informant got via *TITAN*?'

'No, it was a stand-alone platform on the dark web. But they may be using *TITAN* as a marketplace for transactions and important communication, including as a way to run the upcoming auction.' Bec pinned Erica with a serious look. 'This is "need to know" for now. It's tightly held information in case we spook anyone, but the DC wanted me to tell you.'

'That's great news. Thanks, Bec. Is there anything we can do to help you crack it?'

'We need to get our hands on one of the devices. Once we're in, we have to step carefully, not leave any breadcrumbs to reveal we're there or who we are.' Bec smiles thinly. 'But trust me, as soon as I have more information, I'll let you know.'

Chapter 18

Superintendent Greg Hewson, the head of the Murrumbidgee District, is an old friend of Sergeant Mick Peters, who ran the station in Laura's hometown of Wallaby Rock. This mutual connection has helped to build a good rapport over the phone, even before Laura leaves for Griffith. He's already offered valuable insights into the subversive but far-reaching activities of the Australian mafia and welcomed the idea of Laura and Ki spending a few days with him to delve deeper into Sophie Romano's life.

On the long drive, she listens to songs Sophie recorded before she vanished. The missing woman has an ethereal, almost Celtic sound, like a younger version of Annie Lennox, and before long, Laura's decided she's a fan. The potential loss of such an amazing young talent is appalling.

It's late afternoon when Laura rolls into Griffith, but not so late that she doesn't have time for a handful of meetings with Superintendent Hewson and his officers who filed the missing person report for Sophie Romano. While Hewson had already sent Laura transcripts, taped interviews and files to read before leaving – enough to make her head spin – it's good to have face-to-face access to the key players in the investigation. Between them, they decide she and Ki will visit the winery the next day to talk to the owners and staff who worked with Sophie, before conducting a sweep of the property.

She and Ki spend the night with Hewson and his wife, Margot. The couple welcome them with genuine country hospitality. It reminds Laura so much of home and her heart yearns for simpler, happier times. Margot prepares a delicious meal of lamb cutlets and roasted vegetables and tops it off with a homemade chocolate mousse. Laura leaves nothing on the plate.

Over dinner, they discuss Sophie and the impact her disappearance has had on the area.

'Something like this makes everyone jittery,' Hewson confides. 'Around here, kids still ride or walk to school and hang out with their friends playing backyard footy and cricket until the sun goes down. But Sophie's disappearance has shaken families across the district.'

'What about the Romanos. How are they doing now?' Laura asks as she accepts a glass of wine from Margot.

'Oh, poor Paul and Regina. It's a parent's worst nightmare,' Margot responds, her voice shaky. 'There are plenty of people around here who are jealous of their money and success, but they are normal, everyday folk. Salt of the earth and one of the nicest couples you'd ever meet. They personally support many local charities and are actively involved in the community. Sophie was their only child. Naturally, they're at their wits' end.'

After dinner, Margot bids them goodnight and Hewson and Laura move to the living room where Laura switches the conversation to the owners of the winery where Sophie performed. Ki follows them and curls at her feet.

'How well do you know Robert and Joan Larson?' Laura starts.

'I've known them since I transferred from Tamworth over 15 years ago. Their wine is excellent, in fact, this is one of theirs,' he says, holding up the bottle they've been sharing., 'They've won several awards, and the vineyard is a popular spot for weddings and functions, but they've had some difficult times.'

'Difficult? In what way?' Laura asks, sipping from the glass and savouring the delicately balanced flavours. It is a good drop.

'Lots of businesses suffered during COVID, including them. Then there was the lawsuit. One of their staff had a serious accident during harvest and it cost them dearly.'

'But obviously they've overcome those challenges, and they're still going strong?'

Hewson pauses before responding, 'Yes. They were tossed a lifeline from their bank but for a while there, Rob was hunting around town for a new business partner. Someone to get them out of their mess. Rob can be,' again he pauses, 'a prickly customer.

He has a hot temper and can fly off the handle at the slightest provocation. Best to approach him gently tomorrow.'

'Thanks for the tip,' Laura says as she tries to stifle a yawn and rises from the couch. 'I'm sorry, it was a long drive and day. Thank you again for putting us up. Please let Margot know that dinner was delicious. I'll see you in the morning.'

'Bright and early,' he replies.

There's a heavy mist hanging over the vines as they pull in at the cellar door, the foggy blanket deadening any noise in the crisp country air; the strange silence unnerves Laura, and she finds herself a little on edge as she releases Ki from the vehicle.

A woman in her early forties is waiting for them. Her blonde hair is tied in a short ponytail. She's wearing a black pantsuit and a long camel-coloured wool coat that billows behind her as she strides toward them.

Laura looks at Hewson, whose expression, like hers, is questioning, even mystified.

Whoever this is, it's not someone the superintendent arranged for them to meet.

'Superintendent Hewson?' the woman says. 'And this must be Senior Constable Murray and PD Ki. Nice to meet you.' She holds out her hand. 'Detective Alexandra Jeffries. Alex.'

Laura frowns as Jeffries and Hewson shake hands.

'I'm sorry, Detective,' Hewson says, beating Laura to the punch. 'I wasn't informed of your arrival.'

'My apologies, Sir,' Jeffries replies. 'I've just been assigned to Taskforce Lacuna, and Leading Senior Constable Martin told me Constable Murray was coming up here digging for clues into Sophie Romano's disappearance. I wanted to be here. Check out what you turn up, so I headed up here yesterday afternoon. Got in too late for introductions.'

'Indeed,' Hewson says. 'Glad you could join us.'

Jeffries turns her attention to Laura. 'I read your critique of Detective Ryan's assessment, and your additional case notes. You have good instincts. You're wasted in the dog squad.'

Laura opens her mouth to reply, but Jeffries ploughs on. 'Let's go. Daylight's wasting. I've already met the owners and they're expecting you.' Without waiting, she turns and leads the way to an expansive shed at the back of the main building. Signs by the doors indicate this is the home of both the office and wine-making facility.

As she walks behind Jeffries, heat flushes Laura's face and she has to work hard to push down the anger bubbling up inside her. *She's* the one who's built the relationship with Superintendent Hewson and the local team. *She's* the one who's been able to secure a meeting with the owners. Not Detective *'Look at me. I'm so bloody brilliant,'* Alexandra Jeffries.

But if Laura's learned one thing in her short time in the force, it's that some senior officers like to bait junior staff. It's like a game or a power play for them, and when it happens, the best way to nip it in the bud is not to react. Don't give them what they want. If she bites her tongue and ignores Jeffries' superior attitude, she'll soon get bored.

Jeffries reaches the door and holds it open for Laura and Hewson. 'After you.'

Inside, a man and woman in their early sixties are waiting. Both are dressed in jeans, thick fleecy jackets and beanies, and wear knee-length gum boots.

'Morning, Greg,' the man says with clear familiarity.

'Rob,' Hewson replies. 'Joan. Thanks for giving us access to your property again.'

Laura fills in the gaps from her knowledge of the case files and Hewson's inside information. Rob and Joan Larson, second-generation wine growers and owners of the vineyard. She hangs back a little with Ki as the couple lead Hewson and Jeffries out of the building again and begin a short walk around the winery. Her eyes sweep the rolling hills full of vines, her focus split between getting the lie of the land and following the conversation.

'She was such a lovely girl and so talented,' Joan says mournfully. 'She was very popular with visitors to the vineyard and with our staff. She was like a part of the family,'

'Sophie entertained guests, is that right?' Jeffries asks.

'Yes,' Rob replies. 'She sang and played guitar on the weekends. Mostly covers, but she also played some of her own compositions. Like Joan said, she was very talented.'

'How long had Sophie worked here?' Laura asks as they stride toward the vines.

'She'd been performing for about 18 months,' Rob says. 'Pretty much as soon as we reopened for wine tasting and functions. You know, post-COVID.'

'That must have been a difficult time for you,' Jeffries says, her voice warm and sincere. 'Lockdowns must have been hell for you, financially and emotionally.'

'It was a trying time, that's for sure,' Rob replies. 'We had to let staff go, and online sales were the only thing keeping us afloat. When borders and business opened up, we brought Sophie on as an added incentive to get people in the door.'

'But you survived. Financially, I mean.'

'Barely.'

'Still, that's a big achievement, especially with one of your staff suing you for a major workplace injury.'

Laura glances at Jeffries, reevaluating her. She is good. Laura only learned about the lawsuit from Superintendent Hewson last night.

Rob stops at the fence bordering the vines and faces Jeffries. His voice is cold when he responds. 'The case was settled out of court.'

'For a quarter of a million dollars. That's a lot of money to cough up, especially when you're getting back on your feet. How'd you manage it?'

Rob glances at his old friend Superintendent Hewson, who nods at Detective Jeffries, encouraging the vineyard owner to respond. Jeffries stares into the winemaker's face. He returns her steady gaze.

Joan sniffles into a tissue and blows her nose.

'We drew on what was left of our savings and extended our loan with the bank,' he says at last, his face flushing and voice rising. 'But I don't understand what any of that has to do with Sophie.'

'I was just curious,' Jeffries says, smiling. 'We'd like to speak to any staff who worked with Sophie.'

The sudden change of direction unbalances Rob for a second. 'Most of them aren't here. It's midweek, and we only have a skeleton crew Monday to Wednesday.'

'The cellar door's open Thursdays to Sundays,' Joan chips in. 'That's when we're fully staffed.'

'Can we get a copy of the roster for the last weekend Sophie worked, and for the Sunday she never made it?'

'Of course,' Joan squeaks.

'And we'll need the contact details for any staff not here today so we can chat to them later.' Jeffries indicates Laura and

Ki. 'Now, Senior Constable Murray and her police dog would like to look over the grounds, if that's convenient.'

Rob's eyes narrow. He gestures toward the rows of vines stretching out before them, 'Our wine is organic. That means no preservatives and organic farming techniques. It took years to get certification. We don't allow people to wander around willy-nilly and risk any contamination.'

'Naturally,' Jeffries replies, smiling reassuringly. 'Senior Constable Murray and her police dog are highly trained. They'll be very careful. There'll be no *willying* or *nillying*, I'm sure.'

Rob hesitates, then nods.

'I'd like to start with the area where Sophie performed,' Laura says, and Rob points her to an outdoor wine tasting and dining space at the side of the main cellar door.

'We'll get out of your way then,' Jeffries declares, and gestures for the couple and Superintendent Hewson to accompany her back to the office. As they head off, Laura breathes a sigh of relief that she can finally get down to business.

She leads Ki back to the car and grabs something from the back seat. The evening before, Hewson had given her a soft angora jumper that belonged to Sophie – a source of her scent to help Ki track her.

Her canine partner buries his nose in the fluffy material, then they start their inspection of a cobblestone alfresco area under a wisteria-covered pergola. Wine barrel tables and stools are bordered by low flower beds, with a selection of small and long tables dotted throughout the space. Large French doors lead to the cellar door and shop, and in a corner under the wisteria stands the compact wooden platform where Sophie would have played guitar and sung for visitors. The place has a relaxed and friendly vibe, and Laura imagines how delightful it would be to sit in the sunshine, surrounded by the scent of spring blossoms, enjoying a cheese platter and a glass of wine while listening to Sophie's voice.

Ki works his way through the space, and when they get to the stage, he sniffs this way and that before lifting his head and staring at Laura. She swears he looks disappointed.

'It's okay, boy, it was always a long shot,' she says. 'Let's check out the rest of the place.'

By lunchtime, they've completed a full sweep of the property but have had no hits. Disappointed, Laura heads back to the car to return Ki to his crate, only to find Jeffries waiting for her. Needed back at the station, a patrol car had picked up Superintendent Hewson a short while ago.

'Any luck?' the detective asks.

'Nothing.'

'Well, it's not been a complete waste of time,' Jeffries declares tactlessly. 'I spoke to two workers in the shed this morning who were definitely upset about Sophie's disappearance but clammed up when I wanted to discuss Rob and Joan or the business. I've already called Leading Senior Constable Martin to update her, and she's arranging for an analyst to dig into the Larsons' financial records.

'There's something rotten in the state of Denmark, and I'm going to poke around until I find out what it is.'

By the end of the next day, Laura's opinion of Alex Jeffries has entirely thawed.

The detective spends the morning interviewing three casual staff who weren't at the winery the day before – all of them women, aged 25 to 51, and all of whom considered themselves good friends of Sophie's. All three get teary when they talk about Sophie's disappearance, and Laura can't help but be impressed by the subtle way Alex builds a connection with each of them, finding common ground and winning their trust before pressing them about the winery's operations and what it's like working for the Larsons.

The oldest interviewee, Janet, says she's worked for Rob and Joan for seven years, and while her hours were reduced during COVID, she was grateful to be retained by the couple to fill online orders.

'Times were tough,' she says. 'And they weren't made any easier by that stupid lawsuit.'

'You don't believe the compensation claim was justified?' Alex asks.

'Justified? It was just some idiot looking for a quick payout because they were too incompetent to follow WHS guidelines and got themselves hurt. Their stupidity almost got all of us laid off.'

Alex sits back and lets her talk; it's clear Janet has wanted to get this all off her chest for a while but lacked the audience.

'It was terrible for Rob and Joan, put a massive strain on their marriage. Right in the middle of all this, Joan told me she thought the winery wouldn't survive another month, what with the lawsuit and loss of income. Then …'

'Then?' Alex prompts.

'Well, they found an answer just in time. Couldn't have been more than a week later, it was like a weight had been lifted from her shoulders. She was smiling and even laughing again. Seems the bank had agreed to extend their loan to cover everything.'

'Were you surprised?' Alex asks. 'That the bank would pump more money into a business in financial strife?'

'Not really.' Janet frowns, the lines between her eyebrows deepening. 'There was a lot of pressure on banks not to foreclose on businesses because of COVID. It was all over the news.'

With the staff interviews finished, Alex and Laura debrief Superintendent Hewson on what they've learned, and Alex confirms they're getting approval for an analyst to dig into the Larsons' finances. Then they head out for the last and most difficult interview they have to do before heading back to Sydney.

The Romano farm reminds Laura of her old home in Wallaby Rock, except the homestead is nothing short of magnificent. The beautifully restored farmhouse sits on an expansive rice-growing property and is effortlessly charming in the afternoon light.

Alex and Laura accept the offer of coffee.

Sophie's parents usher them into an opulent sitting room. Framed photos of draft horses pulling ploughs with Sophie's ancestors in the foreground and maps of the property hang from a picture rail that rings the room. Ornate ceiling roses showcase the house's heritage, and while the room, like the rest of the house, retains many of its original, character features, it has been tastefully redecorated with furniture and pieces that look like they're out of the pages of *Vogue Living*. As Mr Romano explains the significance of the photos and maps to Alex, Laura comments on the beauty of their surroundings.

'You have a stunning property and home, Mrs Romano,' Laura says as she accepts a plate of tiny cakes from Sophie's mother.

'Thank you,' Mrs Romano smiles her appreciation and Laura notices her eyes are the same shape and colour as Sophie's. The same kindness radiates from her face that jumped out at Laura from her daughter's photo.

'It's been in Paul's family for many generations. We consider ourselves guardians of the property, you know, for the next generation. But Sophie,' Mrs Romano's voice shakes and her husband moves behind her, grasping her shoulders, 'is our only child. We tried for years for more. Without Sophie, there's no one to hand this over to now.'

'We understand how difficult this must be for you both,' Alex starts as she takes a seat on a plush armchair opposite the couple, 'but we'd like to go over the statements you provided, see if we can uncover something new.'

Mr Romano releases his grip on his wife's shoulders and sits next to her on an expansive cream coloured lounge.

'You said there'd been no significant changes in Sophie's behaviour leading up to her disappearance, is that correct?'

'Yes. She was the same as always. Excited about finishing school and hoping to get into the National Institute of Dramatic Arts. It was her dream to study at NIDA and become a successful actor and singer,' Mr Romano replies as his wife wipes away tears.

'And was she dating anyone at the time?'

Mrs Romano glances at her husband before responding. 'No. She's had a few boyfriends over the years but her last relationship was with another girl from school. She was very open with us about her sexuality. Early this year, she told us she was interested in both boys and girls. We love our daughter and have always had a positive and honest relationship with her, but to answer your question, no, she wasn't dating anyone when she went missing.'

'Did she cop some heat about her sexuality? From her friends or teachers? I mean, she attended a co-ed Catholic school, it's not something they usually encourage,' Alex probes.

'She and Bec, the girl she dated for a while, did get harassed by some of the boys. They taunted them, left lewd notes and sex toys in their lockers. It was outrageous behaviour from a small group of *boof-head* boys who probably felt that Sophie and Bec being together was somehow an attack on their masculinity. We and Bec's parents spoke to the school and the boys were suspended and things improved, but it did put a strain on their relationship,' Mrs Romano says and Laura's respect for Sophie's mother goes up a notch.

Alex edges forward in the armchair, leaning into the couple. 'Is that why it ended between them? Was it a messy breakup?'

'No. In the end, it petered out as these things sometimes do, especially when you're young. Sophie was sad for a while but also realistic. Bec wanted to stay in town and was enrolled to become an aged care worker. But as we said, Sophie had big dreams,' Mr Romano replies.

'Do you think any of the boys who were suspended held a grudge? Maybe one of them wanted to prove a point still?'

'I don't think so. They had their fun, took their punishment and it was done. I gave the local police their names when they asked the same questions and I understand they were on a group holiday in Bali at the time.'

Alex leans back in the chair and nibbles at a piece of lemon slice before continuing. 'Is there anyone else who may have wanted to hurt Sophie or was even infatuated with her? Or is there someone who may have wanted to hurt you by getting to Sophie? A disgruntled relative, employee or business partner?'

'No. We've racked our brains to try and think who could have done this. I mean, there are always people ready to tear others down – the tall poppy syndrome – you know what I mean. But all our employees are like family; they're loyal and have been with us for years and our business is owned and operated by us,' Mr Romano replies before his wife nudges him and he continues. 'We watched the interview with Ally Webster's mother and the reward that's been posted. Can you tell us, has it led to any breakthroughs? We're willing to post a significant reward for any information that will help us find Sophie, if you think it will help.'

'I'm sorry, I can't discuss details of another case with you, but if you wanted to post a reward, it may help. It will bring out the vultures and the crazies but it may sway someone who has real information but is unsure about coming forward to do so. While we discuss that some more, Senior Constable Murray and her police dog would like to look at Sophie's room and check out the house and the grounds. Is that okay?'

'Yes, of course. I'll show you where Sophie's room is,' Mrs Romano says, pushing herself up from the lounge.

Their footsteps echo on the polished wood floor as they walk down a long hallway to Sophie's bedroom and Laura shares with Mrs Romano that she has listened to Sophie's music. 'I downloaded Sophie's songs. They're very good, she's immensely talented.'

'Thank you. She is,' Mrs Romano replies and up close, Laura notices dark smudges under her eyes that makeup can't hide and deep lines of worry etched on her face. Pushing open the door to Sophie's bedroom is like entering what Laura imagines is a physical manifestation of the personality of the missing young woman. A huge bookcase crammed with books and record albums takes up one side of the room opposite an enormous four-poster bed adorned with soft, sheer material and fairy lights. Along the window, which overlooks a pretty back garden, is a desk, monitor, laptop, pens and a spiral-bound notepad. Moving to the desk, Laura flicks through the pages of the notepad and reads what she assumes are song titles and lyrics in neat handwriting and smiles when she sees some of the words are scribbled out, with new phrases below and a love heart scrawled next to the final lines. One wall is covered in framed t-shirts from bands and musicians and jammed into a corner is a record player, music stands, a beautiful black acoustic guitar and a smaller electric guitar. Lying on the floor is a small, scratched guitar covered in peeling and faded stickers.

Mrs Romano points to it, 'That was Sophie's first guitar. She was only five and could barely wrap her arms around it. Her other guitars were like an extension of her; she never went anywhere without them. They were with her in the car when –' her voice falters and trails off.

'Thank you, Mrs Romano, I'll get PD Ki and look around.'

Sophie's mum nods and leaves Laura to contemplate how lucky Sophie is to have such a loving and supportive family before she returns with Ki.

Sophie's scent is everywhere – in her room, the house, gardens and shed, but the search is futile. Laura thanks the Romanos for their assistance and as they walk to their cars, Alex confirms that everything Mr Romano said about their business and family checks out.

'I already knew the Romanos were above board but I wanted to test his reaction to the question. I can tell you one thing, he doesn't think much of Rob Larson. He said, "…that man may know how to make wine, but he can't balance a budget." When I prodded him further, he revealed that Rob approached him to invest in the business. Before he'd commit to anything, Paul Romano asked for access to the Larsons' finance records, saying he never jumps into anything without careful consideration. Rob refused and apparently lost it, accusing the Romanos of wanting him to fail so they could swoop in and take the winery. Then Paul

Romano heard that they were saved by the bank. He never made a fuss about it as Sophie was so happy there.'

'Superintendent Hewson told me Rob was running around town looking for a business partner and then it all went quiet. So was the bank their only backer after all?' Laura questions as they lean against her car.

Chapter 19

'Hey, Sis! You up for a gig tonight?'

'I can try,' Laura replies. 'I'm on my way home from Griffith, but I'll be back in the city before tonight.' She's sitting at a picnic table outside a roadhouse on the outskirts of Yass, Ki lying at her feet. She and Alex had spent another night hosted by Superintendent Hewson and his wife before heading off in separate cars this morning. When she'd stopped for a break on the drive, she'd seen a missed video call from her sister, Sarah, and after she'd eaten, called her straight back.

'We're playing at the Enmore,' Sarah yells into the phone. Her face is right up close to the screen, making sure she can be heard over the electric thrum of a guitar in the background. A familiar riff cuts across her again; over her shoulder Laura spots Archie – Sarah's fiancé – doing his soundchecks.

A few cars away, a group of teenagers looks across at the noise. Like Laura, they recognise the tune; Sarah's band has developed a devoted and widening fanbase over the last year or so. It won't be long before the Enmore is too small a venue for them.

'Please say you can make it,' Sarah shouts over the music. 'We haven't caught up in months! I'll get you a backstage pass and we can hang out after the show. Besides, I need to chat with you about wedding plans. We have to make this happen sometime. I can't stay engaged forever.' She grins broadly and Laura can't help but return the smile.

'I still can't believe you're getting married. Finally, after all this time. It's so adult of you. And I'd love to come.' She considers a moment. In quieter moments around the taskforce office, Erica's mentioned that she's a fan of the band, and if she's free it would be a rare chance for her to unwind. Maybe her partner Simon would be free too. And then there's Leon. 'Can I bring a friend or two?'

'No problem. Let me know how many tickets you need and I'll leave them at the door.' Sarah leans closer to the phone and winks at Laura. 'One of them a hot date? Don't tell me you've fallen for some hunky, beefcake copper?'

The telltale heat of embarrassment creeps up Laura's neck as she looks around at the teenagers who are sniggering at the conversation. 'We've only had one proper date. He's not uniform but I do work with him. And that's all you need to know for now.'

'Oh no. You don't get away with it that easy. You're blushing! I need a name and a physical description!'

'Maybe you'll meet him tonight,' Laura says with a laugh.

'You like this guy, don't you?'

'Maybe. But I don't want to jinx it.'

Sarah chuckles. 'Well, I can't wait to meet him. I need to check if he's good enough for my little sister.'

'Please don't embarrass me, Sarah. Don't give him a hard time or say anything to Mum and Dad. I mean, there's nothing to tell yet.'

'Of course not,' Sarah grins. The music has stopped in the background, and she whispers. 'Hey, how did your session with Emily go?'

Sarah is one of the few people who knows about Laura's prophetic dreams, and one of the few who understands how much the death of their grandmother, who also had a special gift, has affected her sister. And after hearing about Emily Holland, a sought-after medium who connects people with loved ones who have passed over, Sarah paid for Laura to have a reading. All Laura had to do was book a date.

'It hasn't, not yet,' she admits. 'Work's been crazy and I've had to reschedule a few times. I'm seeing her on Sunday.'

'You know I'll keep hassling you until you do, so don't pike,' Sarah insists as Laura rolls her eyes.

'Sarah!' Archie calls in the background. 'We've gotta go. The van's double parked out front.

'I have to run, Sis. See you tonight. Love you.'

'Love you too, and thanks for the tickets. I'll message you later to confirm numbers.'

Sarah blows Laura a kiss and hangs up.

When she arrives back with the taskforce it's late afternoon and she heads straight to Erica's office. Her boss is on a call but beckons her inside and hangs up within a few moments.

'Welcome back,' she says with a smile. 'Mixed results out Leeton way, I hear.'

Alex works fast, Laura thinks. I've only been back five minutes and Erica's up to speed. Then she remembers the detective had called ahead to clear the investigation of the winery's finances – it would make sense she reported on everything else at the same time. 'Not a wasted trip, though.'

'Not at all.' Erica sits back from the desk. 'What's up?'

'I had a call from Sarah. Her band's playing at the Enmore Theatre tonight. She has some tickets if you'd like to come. Simon's welcome, of course.'

'I'd love to,' Erica says, waving a hand towards her screen. 'I need to get my head out of this for a while. And I'm sure Simon's free. The poor guy's been on night shifts for two weeks and has a couple of days off. He was snoring when I left this morning so he should be refreshed and ready to go.'

'Good,' Laura says. 'I'll let Sarah know.' She remains seated, fidgeting in the chair.

'Something else you want to talk about?' Erica asks. 'Is everything okay?'

'Um … can I ask you something? Something personal?'

'Of course. I was your friend long before I was your boss.'

Touched by the genuine concern on Erica's face, Laura opens up. 'You've had relationships with guys on the force, right? And they haven't turned out … great.'

'That's one way to put it,' Erica says with a rueful smile.

'Do you think it's a mistake to date someone you work with?'

Erica puffs out her cheeks. 'It's not easy. And you're right, it hasn't worked out for me. Remember Tony?' she asks and Laura nods, recalling the last partner Erica had moved in with. They'd been together for over a year before they parted. 'I thought he could be the one, but the pressure of both being in the job was hard to overcome. You can't help but download to each other, but that also means neither of you can escape. Plus, you both know the risks that come with the job and every day you worry if the one you love will make it home. Eventually, it takes a toll, a big toll.

'That doesn't mean it won't work for you, but the job is tough. You understand what I mean?' Erica pauses before continuing, lowering her voice, 'And I know it's scary for you to put yourself out there after … after what you went through with Gary. Can I ask who you're talking about?'

'He's not uniform. He's tech. We've been doing the coffee run together and he's been on some walks with me and Ki.'

'Ah … Leon,' Erica says. 'I'd be lying if I said I hadn't noticed the way he acts around you and the time you two spend together.'

Laura blushes. 'We've only been on one proper date. I think he likes me, but I'm worried about taking that leap. What with the job and everything.'

'He's a great guy, Laura, and he's a civilian. That changes things. His job is full-on and he's involved in some serious stuff, but he doesn't strap on a firearm and put his life on the line like we do. I think he'll be good for you.

'But,' she goes on, 'there are rules about dating other staff. You need to let HR know of any change in your personal circumstances. Just don't let it get in the way of your work, and I think you'll be fine. And no funny business in the office!'

'Oh, God no, I wouldn't do that!' Laura says, embarrassed. 'But I'm going to ask him to come to the show tonight, so I kind of wanted to run it by you first.'

Erica grins. 'Well, I hope he's a fan of loud, indie music.'

Laura finds Leon alone in the staff room, punching a button on the vending machine for a caffeine-loaded soft drink. 'C'mon, don't do this again,' he mutters and slams his hand into the side of the machine.

'Probably easier to go out for a coffee,' Laura says. He jumps and she realises he'd been so absorbed in battling the machine, he didn't hear her come in. 'Sorry, I didn't mean to scare you.'

'It wasn't the jolt I came in here for,' he replies, beaming at her. 'Welcome back! And no, I didn't feel like a coffee run. Hasn't been the same.'

Erica's warning about public displays of affection rings in her ears, and she resists the urge to wrap her arms around him. Instead, she moves closer to the machine and hits the button hard with the base of her palm. A can rattles to the dispensing tray. 'Voila.'

'How can I ever repay you?' Leon teases, bowing to her.

'Well …' Laura says, pretending to think about it, 'you could keep me company tonight at a gig. My sister's band is playing at the Enmore and I've got free tickets.'

'She's in a band big enough to play there? You just said she was a bit of a muso. What are they called?'

'Waiting for Tomorrow.'

'Get out!' Leon almost shouts. 'Are you serious? Your sister is Sarah Murray? The keyboard player? I can't believe I didn't make the connection.'

'Oh, so you know them.'

'Know them? They dominate my playlists!' He's almost vibrating with excitement; Laura wonders if he might explode. 'I'd love to go! And I'm happy to pay for my ticket.'

'Hey, tickets are free. It's one of the perks of being related to a rock star. I've asked Erica and her partner Simon to come too. I hope that's okay. There'll be no shop talk, I promise.'

'Yeah, sure, no problem. Do you want me to pick you up or do you want to meet at the theatre? Or…' he leans forward and gazes into her eyes, '…maybe you'd like to get some dinner in the city before the show?'

Laura runs her fingers along his arm. Their faces are almost touching now. 'Dinner would be great. I know a cute tapas bar near the theatre. I'll send you the details. I'll meet you at seven?'

'I can't wait.'

Chapter 20

The night out goes better than Laura could have hoped. As they polish off tapas and oysters, she and Leon talk about anything and everything, all the way back to their childhoods.

'My mum moved here from Sri Lanka with my grandparents in the mid-80s,' Leon says, sipping his wine. 'She was only 19 when she met my dad. They were at a mutual friend's party, with dates, when they just hit it off. It wasn't long before they were married and my twin sisters came along; I didn't show up until later.'

'I didn't know you had siblings.'

'Sure do. Nicky is a psychologist and Natalie is a school principal. Don't see as much of them as I used to, unfortunately. Dad was a policeman; he died of a heart attack when I was in Year 12.

'Mum struggled. Went into a deep depression, so I stayed living with her after school. I wanted to be there to support her, but it also helped me save a deposit for my own place. Anyway, she started seeing this new guy about six months ago. He's from some small town down south, and she's seriously considering leaving Sydney to be with him.' He laughs. 'So, I guess now is the right time to move out, huh?'

Laura regards him over the top of her drink. He's opening up more than any guy has before, making himself vulnerable and she feels compelled to reciprocate. That hasn't happened in the longest time.

'Well, it was life on the farm for me,' she says. 'Hanging out with Sarah and getting into trouble exploring the bush. You know I wanted to be a vet until …'

Leon gives her a moment. 'Until you met Erica and she became your role model.'

'Yes.' She hesitates. She knows what she needs to talk about next, but she's never really shared it with anyone outside her closest family and friends. That she's even considering doing so tells her how important Leon is becoming in her life. 'Can I tell you something? Something in confidence?'

Leon stretches across the table and places his fingers over hers. 'Yes, you can.'

'You know about what happened in Wallaby Rock. The Bush Basher?'

'Of course.'

'I knew him. Gary Wilson. The Bush Basher. My testimony helped put him in prison.'

Leon's eyes widen. 'No way.' He does some mental arithmetic. 'But you'd only have been…'

'I'd just finished school.' She hesitates an instant, then takes the plunge, 'Gary murdered Benny and Jordy Thompson. They were the brothers of my best friend, Joanna. We used to hang out and train together. Gary was twisted. He killed them as a way of avenging his ancestor, who was the archenemy of Joanna's forebear. But he enjoyed it so much he went on to murder Yvette Berger – I didn't know her; she worked at a nearby orchard – then killed Mia Stevens. Mia and I went to primary school together.'

Laura swirls the wine in her glass, transfixed by the light from the candle as it shines through the pale-yellow liquid. 'Only a few people know what I'm about to tell you and I'd like to keep it that way.'

'No problem,' Leon says, his face serious. He's still holding her hand across the table.

'Gary tried to get me too. I was his next target. I told Erica about an encounter I had with him and it helped to secure the search warrant that led to his arrest.' Still, she holds back; she's not ready to tell him about her gift, her dreams.

'Far out, Laura. That's intense.' His fingers intertwine with hers. 'Thank you for telling me. I swear I won't share what you said with anyone.'

'Thank you,' she murmurs. 'It's made it difficult for me to …'

'To what?'

'To trust anyone.' She looks deep into his eyes. 'To … form a lasting relationship.'

He returns the gaze, and all she can see is absolute sincerity. 'You can trust me.' It's his turn to hesitate. 'I've only had two serious girlfriends, neither lasted more than six months. And that was down to me, not them. After dad died … well, I was the man of the house, as well as studying. And then there was my career. I didn't have the focus for a relationship. I wasn't ready. I am now.' Laura squeezes his hand. 'I like you, Laura. A lot. I get so nervous around you, there are times I can't string two words together. What I am trying to say is, you can trust me. Because I want to keep seeing you more than anything ... you know, if you want to.'

A warmth blossoms inside Laura, like the spring sun softening frost-covered ground, and a tingling sensation spreads across her skin. Giving in to impulse and ignoring the other diners, she rises from her seat, leans across the table and kisses him. 'I'd like that very much.' They leave the restaurant, hand in hand.

Laura's nose wrinkles at the familiar smell of disinfectant. Somewhere a machine pings monotonously, the sound reverberating down the empty hallway. Harsh fluorescent light makes the faded paint on the walls look even more washed out. There's a crucifix above the doorway.

112

She knows this place. Remembers it.

This is where Gran left them.

A nurse bustles past her and goes into the room with the cross over the door. Laura follows her in.

Gran lies motionless in bed, tubes sprouting from her scarecrow-thin arms. Her skin sags around her face. The nurse checks her blood pressure before recording some notes on a chart that she hangs over the end of the bed.

'How's she doing, nurse?' a man asks from the doorway. Laura turns to face him. It's Simon, Erica's partner.

Laura's only known him a short time; how can he be here, now, with Gran?

'No change, doctor,' the nurse answers. 'Her BP is dropping and she's still unresponsive.'

Simon walks to the side of the bed. Leaning over the fragile woman, he places a stethoscope in his ears and checks her heart. Next, he pinches her skin and lifts her eyelids, shining a tiny torch into each pupil before joining the nurse to examine the chart.

As he does so, Gran's eyes fly open and her gnarled fingers point to him. Her mouth stretches wide, turning inside out as it swallows her face, revealing sharp, white teeth and a deep, dark tunnel. The voice that emanates from its depths is Gary's.

'Remember. I'm not the only one!'

Laura jerks awake, her hands and face clammy, heart pounding. Disoriented and fumbling in the dark, her trembling hands find the light switch.

It takes a moment to remember where she is – Erica's spare bedroom.

There's a half-empty bottle of water and a packet of Panadol on the floor beside her. Her clothes are in a messy pile in the corner next to her handbag and she's in an oversized t-shirt she borrowed from Erica.

Images crystallise slowly in her head. Arriving at the theatre holding hands with Leon, prompting a quick, subtle wink from Erica. Erica introducing them to Simon. Grabbing their tickets and being shown to a spot near the front of the stage, singing and dancing to the music, then meeting the band after the show. Leon gushing when he's introduced to the group. All four of them kicking on with Sarah and Archie to a nearby hotel. Simon convincing them both to stay at their place for the night. Leon declining but sneaking a long kiss with Laura before climbing into a taxi.

But the pleasant experience of reliving that kiss is swept away by her recollection of that dream. What the hell *was* that? Gran, Simon and a warning from Gary?

She has long accepted her nighttime visions can contain important messages but she's never had one this bizarre. She can rationalise Gran's presence because she'd been thinking about her when she fell asleep, mulling over how much she would have liked Leon, and picturing how excited she would be about Sarah's wedding.

Same for Simon. He's obviously appeared in her head because she's spent the night talking to him. So how did all that mash into Gran/Gary pointing him out as … what? Evil? Laura hasn't known him that long, but she knows he's well respected in his work, and he makes Erica happier than Laura's ever seen.

Her temples are pounding and her mouth parched, so she pops two headache tablets, washing them down with the last of the water. The nightmare has to be a result of too much booze; not every dream she has means something. Shaking her head, she creeps to the toilet.

As she walks back to bed, she passes a small room on her right, its door ajar. Something makes her stop, peer through the gap. The space beyond glows with the soft light of a streetlamp peeking through the blinds. There's a long oak desk, on which sits an expensive-looking monitor, keyboard and banker's lamp. Behind it is a white leather office chair, and a small filing cabinet and bookcase crammed with medical books and journals take up the rest of the space.

Instinct makes Laura step inside and close the door behind her. She slips across to the desk and flicks on the lamp.

What am I doing?

Proving to yourself the dream was just a dream. That there's nothing suspicious about Simon.

She almost believes herself.

She tries the cabinet first – locked – then switches on the computer.

Password protected.

Turning, she faces the bookcase and takes down papers and books, fanning out pages, before replacing them. Sitting on the middle shelf is Simon's medical degree, displayed in a beautiful, oversized frame that seems to have been handcrafted from the same oak as the desk. Laura picks it up to admire the workmanship, and her fingers touch something poking out at the back. She turns the frame around and discovers a tiny velvet pouch has been tucked into the edge of it.

She wriggles it free and opens it. It contains a key.

Hands trembling, she takes it to the cabinet and tries the lock. It opens to reveal neatly filed notebooks and papers. Pushing hanging files aside, her fingers scrabble along the lining of the cabinet. The edge lifts at her touch and she eases it up, finding a folder has been slipped into the gap. She slides it free and opens it, finding several loose pages of what look like coordinates.

She curses herself for not having her phone and is pondering what to do when there's the sharp noise of coughing from the main bedroom. Easing the folder back into position, she locks the cabinet, turns off the monitor and shoves the pouch with the key into the back of the frame. After switching off the lamp, she steps into the corridor, leaving the study door slightly open, just as she'd found it. Without looking back, she hurries to her room.

She moves so quickly, she doesn't notice the door to the main bedroom close softly.

Chapter 21

It's been a long time since Erica let loose like that, and Simon and Laura looked equally rough this morning. Laura hardly spoke a word before dashing out the door, refusing their offer of bacon and eggs, saying she was too hungover to even stomach breakfast. Plus, she said, she needed to get home to feed Ki, who'd been left alone all night.

Instead of cooking then, Erica decides on splurging and takes Simon to a local café for brunch. It takes a little while – and some strong coffee – before they can form complete sentences enough to talk about the night before.

'God, how long has it been since we've done something that crazy?' Erica asks, having polished off her plate of eggs.

'Forever,' Simon replies. 'Laura and Leon are cute together. They been together long?'

'They hang out at work a lot, but they'd only been on one real date before last night. But you saw them. Holding hands, sneaking kisses – I'd say they're official.'

'So, Leon's on the taskforce too?'

'Hey,' Erica admonishes. 'This is our first day off together in ages. No work talk.'

'I know but I can't resist a blossoming love story.'

'You're such a romantic. Yes, Leon's on the team too. He's a tech guru. A real asset to the team. And a great guy, obviously.'

'Sounds like Laura has snagged a good one.'

'She has but so has he. I hope it works out for her.'

'Hey, all you can do is support them … both as a friend and a boss.'

'Enough about them,' Erica says. 'What on earth are we going to do with a whole day free?' The prospect of it thrills her. No doubt about it, Simon has changed her life. Before him, she'd never had a partner who could put up with her demanding hours and tough job, not even her former partner Tony. She yearned for someone who would listen, share their feelings, treat her with respect and put her first when needed, but a guy like that seemed rarer than unicorns. She grins and rubs his leg under the table with her foot. 'Any ideas?'

'I'm sure we'll think of something,' Simon replies, and waves to the server for the bill.

Chapter 22

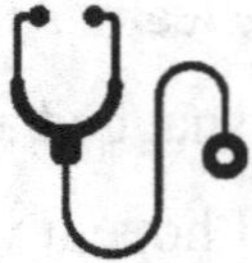

The large sign directing patients and visitors to Parramatta District Hospital is hard to miss, yet Simon drives by it. He continues for another 15 kilometres, taking side roads and detours before finally parking in a visitor space outside a large hotel in Fairfield.

The glass doors slide open and he nods at the concierge behind the desk as he strides to the hotel restaurant, where a statuesque and busty blonde is seated at a table. He moves to her side, kisses her cheek and takes a seat opposite.

'You're late,' she says, tapping her long, tapered nails on her phone.

'I had to wait for the right time to slip away. Wanted to make sure I wasn't being followed.' Simon sits back from the table as a waiter materialises to pour fresh coffee into his cup.

'What do you mean, the right time?' the woman asks when the server has moved away. 'You're a doctor. Just tell her you have an emergency to go to. Or maybe,' she snarls, 'you didn't want to get out of bed and leave your precious Erica.'

'You know that's —'

'Don't forget where your loyalties lie. Who's paying for your degree, Dr. Russell? You owe us. You owe *me*.'

Simon lets that go. It's not a wise move to antagonise her further. 'I'm here now. With you. Besides, I have important news.'

'Well, I have something important I need to tell you too,' the woman says as she reaches under the table and places his hand on the inside of her thigh. 'But I think we should talk about it in private, don't you?'

Her moods give him whiplash, but he's learned to adapt to them. He drains his almost-full cup of coffee, before pushing back his seat and heading to the lobby, the elevator, and her room.

Chapter 23

The front steps are cracked and worn and pieces of the wood lacework framing the verandah are missing, but the old home has character. The rambling roses covering the arch to the red-brick cottage, however, remind Laura of Gran, and for a moment she thinks about backing out. But she's already booked, cancelled and rebooked. Today, she's going to go through with it.

Chewing on the inside of her bottom lip, she reaches for the doorbell.

When it swings open, all Laura can do is stare, unable to speak. The woman who answered has greying hair tied in a loose bun and blue-grey eyes just like her grandmother.

'Hello, Laura,' she says. 'I wasn't sure if you'd turn up but I'm glad you did. I'm Emily. Please, come in.'

'Thank you,' Laura manages to say as she continues to gawk. 'I'm sorry about stuffing you around. It was hard to find a time to come.'

'I understand,' Emily says, as she leads the way to a sitting room. There's a piano in one corner, two armchairs covered in a worn floral brocade face each other, and a matching two-seater couch is positioned along the wall. A round, low coffee table stands to one side of the armchairs. 'Would you like a cup of tea or coffee before we start? I've just made a pot of tea for myself if you want one.'

Laura breathes in the aroma of Irish Breakfast and chokes back unexpected tears. 'Thank you. A cup of tea would be lovely.'

Emily motions to Laura to take a seat in one of the chairs, then bustles away to the kitchen and starts rattling cups.

Ignoring the proffered chair, Laura instead remains standing, examining the photos lining the top of the piano. She's so engrossed that she doesn't hear Emily return.

'They're my children, Michael and Thomas,' the old woman says, 'their wives and my grandchildren.' She carries a tray bearing a teapot, two cups and matching saucers, which she places on the coffee table.

Laura picks up a photo of a toddler with vibrant, red curly hair and bright blue eyes. The child is holding a small teddy bear and giggling in the picture.

'That's Posie, my newest grandchild. She's a handful but such a sweetheart. Why don't you take a seat and we'll get started.' She pours tea into the delicate porcelain cups.

Laura sits on the edge of the armchair and picks up a cup. She sips the hot tea and replaces it on the table with a loud clatter onto the saucer. 'Sorry,' she mutters as tea splashes onto the table.

'It's okay, Laura. I can feel your nerves. They're pouring out of you. Let me put you at ease, explain how this works.' She raises her own cup to her lips, places it down again gently. 'Every medium works differently. Some mediums need to hold something that belonged to the person who has crossed over. Me – I hold your hands and ask you to concentrate. Picture the person you want to reach, visualise them in the room with us.'

Laura nods. Some of her tension eases at how simple it sounds, but she's still on edge.

'For it to work, you need to have a clear intention of who you want to contact and what you want to say or ask,' Emily goes on. 'And you have to be open for it to be successful. Is that something you can manage?'

'I think so,' Laura says. After all, this wouldn't be her first strange experience.

'Then all I do is close my eyes and hopefully they come. Sometimes it doesn't work. Like I said, it relies on you as much as me. So, who would you like to reach today?'

'Gran,' Laura whispers. 'My grandmother, Grace. She passed away so quickly, and I was so busy with my new job that I never got to tell her how much she means to me. How special she is and how much I love her.'

'Okay then. Are you ready to begin?'

Laura nods again.

'Very well. I want you to breathe deeply and think about Gran. Picture her here with us. Her face, hair, clothes, her smell and mannerisms.' Emily reaches out and grasps Laura's hands gently in hers, then closes her eyes.

Laura does the same and visualises Gran in the room with them; her immaculate make-up, smooth, greying bobbed hair.

Somewhere, a clock ticks.

At last, Emily speaks. 'Your Gran said it's nice you put your face on today.'

Tears fill Laura's eyes at the familiar phrase as Emily continues. 'She said not to fret. She knows you love her. She loves you and misses you, too. She knows you got the medal. You and your dog? She wants you to know she was there. She thought that maybe you realised she was with you. That made her happy.

'She's been trying to reach you, but she says it's been difficult. But she wants you to know she's proud of you and she's happy you've found a nice man. He's a good catch. Smart and handsome, and she says you look good together. She thinks your personalities and looks complement each other, like Yin and Yang. And she wants you to tell Sarah that she'll be there for the wedding, in her heart, and watching on. Can you tell her?'

'Yes,' Laura croaks as tears, like rivers of sadness, stream out of her.

Emily shudders and their joined hands tremble. 'Someone else is trying to reach you. They're very insistent. Is there anyone else you wanted to contact today?'

'No. Just Gran.'

'I'm losing her, Laura. Wait, she's saying something about another one? Something about … family? I'm sorry, she's gone.'

Laura sighs and tries to free her hands, but Emily grips them tighter, fingers digging into her flesh.

'You're not welcome,' she growls. 'Leave now.'

The room has gone cold, and Laura opens her eyes. Emily is shaking her head from side to side.

'I told you. Leave her alone! Go! Get out!'

Abruptly, she releases Laura's hands and opens her eyes. The connection is broken.

'What happened?' Laura asks, her body quivering. There's a box of tissues on the table, and she reaches for one.

Emily breathes deeply and rubs her temples. 'Another presence tried to break in on our communion. He called himself Shadow Man. Does that mean anything to you?'

'Yes,' Laura whispers. She tastes blood in her mouth and realises she's bitten the inside of her lip.

'Such hatred and anger,' Emily says. 'I've never felt anything so cold, so malicious. It took all my willpower to push him away.' She takes Laura's hands again, reassuring. 'But he is what he said, Laura. Shadow and mist. You can stop him.'

Laura finds herself shaking her head, not even meaning to do it.

'No, Laura, you're stronger than you know. I can feel it. You have power – enough to get rid of this man once and for all. Believe in yourself.'

Choking back tears Laura focuses on the floral pattern on the armchair; the freckles on her pale skin stand out like beacons.

'You're special too, aren't you?' Emily says. 'I could sense it in you when we met. A warm, familiar feeling, like there was a connection or bond between us. That we're kindred spirits somehow.'

And without hesitation, Laura opens up, spilling her secret to this stranger. Only the other night, she'd baulked at telling Leon, but here she is, letting it all out to a woman she's only just met.

For some obscure reason, Emily makes her feel comfortable. Safe.

'I've always had dreams,' she says. 'Dreams about things that have happened or things I could never know. Sometimes they're warnings, for me or for other people.'

'And this Shadow Man appears in them?'

'He used to. He murdered my friends and wanted to kill me, but my dreams … my testimony helped to put him in prison. He died there.'

'Yet he's still in your dreams.'

'He wasn't for years, but now he's back. Taunting me and threatening me. Talking about taking revenge.'

'Has Gran been in your dreams too? She said she's been trying to reach you.'

'Yeah. I think she's trying to warn me. About Shadow Man … or someone else? I don't know. Gran had the gift, too,' Laura says, a small smile on her face. She nods at the teacup in front of her. 'She could read tea leaves. She was one of the few people who understood what I was dealing with. But it's like Gary – that was his name – is trying to invade or taint my memories of her. Like he's twisting them to frighten me. Now I don't know whether to listen to my dreams or ignore them.'

'Having a gift like this is a blessing and a curse,' Emily replies. 'Trust me, I know. But it's not something you can disregard. I tried that when I was younger. I didn't want to do this. To *be* this. So, I tried to block it, but that only made it worse. It was like water against a cracked dam; eventually, it burst through.'

'So, what did you do?'

'I learned to be honest with myself. You have to be, too. Learn to embrace and hone your gift but not let it dominate your life. Something like this can take years to master, but with practice you can do it.'

Laura nods as Emily's eyes lock on hers, eyes that remind her so much of her beloved grandmother. It's like somehow a piece of her is still here.

'One last thing,' Emily says. 'The man Gran said you're dating. Does he know about your gift?'

In her head, Laura hears children in the playground shouting out 'Loopy Laura'. She pictures them pointing at her, mocking her, chasing her. 'No. It's too soon.'

'Don't leave it too long,' Emily cautions. 'You need to be open and honest for relationships to blossom. If he cares about you, he'll embrace you. All of you.'

As if to prove Emily's words, there are flowers waiting for Laura on her doorstep, with a note: 'If music be the food of love, play on'. Below it, Leon has put a link to a Spotify playlist.

She carries the flowers inside, where Ki is waiting to greet her. After fussing over him, she starts searching the cupboards for something to hold the bouquet. She selects a large plastic jug and fills it with water, making a mental note to buy a proper vase, then types Leon's link into her phone so she has something to listen to as she arranges the flowers.

The first song is 'Stars in My Eyes' by Ball Park Music, her favourite band. That's followed by 'Date Night' from Sarah's band, Waiting for Tomorrow. The rest of the mix covers everything from 'The Skye Boat Song' – the theme song from

Outlander – to The Beatles, Fleetwood Mac, Madonna, Taylor Swift and Billie Eilish. Grinning, she gives him an A for effort and for paying attention to her likes and dislikes.

After the emotional whirlwind she's experienced with Emily, Leon's modern take on a cute 80s approach to sharing music lifts her spirits, and she pours herself a glass of wine, Ki curling at her feet, before calling him to thank him.

'So, you liked it?' he asks as soon as he picks up.

'I loved it,' Laura replies, Emily's words about being honest and open to allow love to blossom still at the front of her mind. 'Come over?'

'I'd love to,' he replies. 'But only on one condition.'

Chapter 24

By the time Leon arrives bearing a bulging bag of groceries, Laura has the playlist he made for her running in the background, candles are lit, and there's a bottle of wine and glasses on the kitchen bench, with the flowers he bought sitting to one side.

All he has to do is fulfil the agreed condition and cook dinner for her.

As he busies himself in the kitchen, Laura sidles up beside him. She's wearing jeans and an emerald-green jumper, and he can't help thinking what a striking contrast it makes with her fair skin and auburn hair.

'You seem to know your way around a kitchen,' she says, watching him deftly slice a capsicum into strips.

'Mum made sure we all knew how to cook,' he replies. 'We even had rostered nights to prepare dinner. We could cook whatever we wanted, but if we missed one of our nights, we had to make up an extra night the following week.'

'Well, I'm impressed and remind me to thank your mum one day,' Laura says.

'You haven't eaten anything yet.'

After dinner – a spicy chicken and vegetable stir fry with noodles – they sit together on the couch, Laura leaning her head on Leon's shoulder as he wraps his arms around her.

'You smell like strawberries and sriracha,' Leon murmurs.

'Well, the "strawberries" is my shampoo, but I don't know how I got your dinner in my hair,' Laura laughs.

Leon tilts her face to his, entwining his fingers in a loose strand of her hair and kissing her.

Laura pulls away, and his face falls. 'I'm sorry. Am I going too fast?'

'No. I want to, but there's something I need to tell you first.'

Leon caresses her face, waiting for her to speak. She twists her hands in her lap, avoiding his eyes.

'When I told you my testimony put Gary, the Bush Basher, behind bars, I didn't tell you everything.'

'Oh?' he says. He tries to sound calm as he feels her body tense beside him, like she's ready to leap up and run away at any moment.

'I was helped with how I got my information,' she goes on. 'I have … dreams.' She pauses, waiting for a reaction from him but he waits, wanting Laura to tell him whatever has made her so anxious in her own time. 'They show me things I couldn't possibly know. Warnings. Like a kind of second sight. Erica believed me when I told her, and acted on the information to bring Gary in.'

Laura's confession hangs in the air. In the background, the Spotify mix transitions softly to Madonna's 'Borderline'.

Then Leon bursts out laughing.

Laura flushes, her face a storm of shame, humiliation and confusion.

Noticing her hurt expression, Leon stops and gets control of himself. He grasps her hands in his. 'Oh, Laura. I didn't mean to upset you. I'm just so *relieved*. I thought you were going to tell me you had a secret boyfriend back at Wallaby Rock, or that you changed your mind and weren't interested in me.'

He watches as she scans his face, tears in the corners of her eyes. He squeezes her hand, reassuring her, and she smiles back at him.

'I understand this is a big deal,' he says, 'but for me it means you're even more special. And you're going to get on so well with my mum! She's always talking about signs and listening to your inner voice. She'd call you "a wise old soul".' He kisses her on the forehead. 'Thank you. For trusting me with this.'

'There's more,' she says, picking up her wine and twisting the glass back and forth by its stem.

'Go on. You can tell me,' Leon encourages, 'and if you keep that up, your wine will be all over the floor.'

Laura stops playing with the glass and takes a deep breath. 'The night we watched Sarah and the band, I had a dream at Simon and Erica's. Gary – the Bush Basher – he appears in my nightmares sometimes, and his voice came out of my Gran … It was like she was telling me Simon was some kind of threat to me. That I'm in danger.'

'Okay,' Leon says, keeping his voice as neutral as possible.

'And I didn't know what to make of it so I … I searched his office while they were asleep.'

'You did what?'

'I knew you wouldn't –'

'No, I'm not judging!' Leon says quickly. 'I just can't believe how risky that was. Did you find anything?'

'Some weird papers with map coordinates on them, or something. I didn't have my phone, so I couldn't get any pictures.'

'That's a shame,' Leon says. 'I might have been able to work out what they were.'

'You don't think I'm nuts?'

'No,' Leon replies. 'I believe you. But are you sure it means Simon is up to something? Who knows, they could be coordinates to find geocaches.'

'Does Simon look like someone who'd do geocaching to you?' and Leon shakes his head.

'Well, like I said, I didn't know what to make of the dream at first. I thought it was just alcohol, partying and no sleep playing havoc with me. But then Gary turned up again today.'

'Another dream?'

'No. Look, please don't think I'm a total nutcase but I'd gone to visit a medium. Sarah bought me a session with one to help me cope with Gran's passing. But the medium sensed him too – she even knew he called himself the Shadow Man – and she said he was telling her the same thing. That I have to be careful who I trust.' She sighs and rubs her temples. 'Her knowing that really freaked me out. I don't know. Gary was a twisted, evil man, and this is like he's tormenting me again. Haunting me. But I keep thinking that if I'd listened to my dreams five years ago, maybe I could have stopped him earlier. Saved lives. I don't want to make that same mistake again.'

Leon is quiet for a moment, processing. 'You and Erica are friends, not just colleagues,' he says at last. 'You said she believed you and stood up for you before. Tell her what you dreamt and what you found in the study. If she listened then, hopefully she'll listen now.'

Laura's voice catches in her throat, 'But she loves him, Leon. She's never been happier. What if I'm wrong? This will hurt her. It might destroy their relationship. I might wreck our friendship.'

'What do you feel, deep inside? Do you think the dream means something?'

'I wasn't sure before today, but the medium told me to listen to my gift, to pay attention to what I see. I can't ignore this. Can't take the chance that something might happen to her.'

'Then you need to talk to Erica soon.' Leon cups her face and kisses her. 'You are extraordinary, Ms Murray. And I am totally falling for you.'

'You are?'

'I am,' he says as Taylor Swift's 'Lover' comes on the playlist and their lips meet.

Chapter 25

Staring at the numbers on the alarm clock, Dan wills himself to sleep.

But he has nothing to help him settle. He hasn't laid a bet or worked out in weeks. He needs the buzz of a big win or an endorphin hit from exercise. Something other than booze to escape his thoughts.

When Martin had told him Cain Anderson had met with one of the Scorpions, he'd panicked. He'd begged her to get him out, to put him, Ellie and his mum into protection right now. Instead, she'd convinced him to hold on. Said she'd only need his help for a little longer and then he'd be done. He just had to contact Anderson and find out why they didn't get the full time they were promised to view the women, and to say the people he represented wanted in for the auction.

Until then, she guaranteed he and his family would be safe.

Dan had considered doing a runner, must have packed and unpacked his bag six times. If it were just him, he'd go — somewhere, anywhere — but he has to think of Ellie and his mum.

They'd always be on the move and looking over their shoulder. That's no way to raise a kid.

No, Ellie needs the security of witness protection.

So, he'd messaged Anderson as Martin instructed. Apparently, there had been a 'technical problem' with the live feed of the women, but Anderson told him his clients should have seen enough to know the product is good. They wouldn't be getting any more cheap previews. This, Anderson explained, wasn't his call—it was his boss calling the shots.

Dan knew better than to ask who that was. Sticking to his instructions, he'd said his clients were keen to get in on the auction and asked for details about how it will work. In response, Cain had agreed to catch up with him again in a week to confirm the entry fee, as well as when and how to join, and how bidding would work.

Martin had been pleased with his progress, congratulating him on getting them this far and reinforcing how important it was that he stick it out. Once he had the vital information about the auction, she'd told him, he'd be out. He'd have the security of witness protection and a new life with Ellie and his mum.

But every night since then, Dan has wandered the house unable to sleep, creeping around like a mouse, always alert and waiting for the family cat to pounce. He's had to use all his willpower to resist the urge for a hit. He was never a regular user; it wasn't good for business or his health to sample his own merchandise, and he hasn't touched coke or meth since he learned he was going to be a dad. He wanted to set a good example for the kid.

The wait has almost killed him and the meeting with Anderson is still two days away.

He gives up on tossing and turning and rolls out of the covers. If he can't settle his head with booze or drugs, it'll have to be exercise. At this hour, he should have the gym to himself.

He pulls on workout gear, grabs his bag and car keys and picks up his phone. Opening the encrypted app he uses with Martin, he disables it, along with location tracking and Bluetooth. He needs space, not more questions about why he's leaving the house and where he's going in the middle of the night.

Outside the front door, he pauses, peering up and down the street; he spots the unmarked car parked down the road and knows he'll have to lose it. Folding his vast frame into his black Ford Mustang, he's already thinking of how to shake the surveillance.

It's a 10-minute trip to the gym, but it takes Dan more than 40, following round-about routes and speeding down back streets to lose the tail. At last, he's free of them, and circles round again to park at the back of an all-hours gym. It's one of many he frequents, both to work out and as a regular supplier of illegal steroids, coke and ice.

He swipes his membership card and lets himself in through the rear door, calling out to see if anyone is around. A quick check of the bathrooms confirms he's alone, and he stomps past treadmills, step machines and bikes to the nearest rowing machine.

He grabs his towel and dumps his bag before turning on the TV and switching to the music channel. Scantily clad women parade in front of rappers dripping with gold chains and attitude; Dan turns up the volume and starts the rowing program, increasing his speed in time to the beat.

He's slick with sweat by the time he finishes, wiping down the machine and sponging his face, before moving to the weight benches. He flexes his bulging biceps in the mirror before selecting some gigantic weight plates and setting them on each end of the barbell, then powders his hands before stretching out, his legs bent on either side of the bench, a towel under his head. Grunting, he pushes the weights into the air, pulling them back to his chest and repeating this 12 times before resting the bar in the cradle and taking a breather. Deciding he needs more of a challenge, he adds more weight to each side, the metal clanking into place before he powders his hands again and resumes his position. Gripping the metal, he groans as he eases the bar above him ... then his breath rushes out in a loud *whoof* as the massive load comes down hard on his chest.

Two burly men have taken position, one on either side of the barbell, and hold it down on Dan's sternum. The enormous pressure almost cracks his bones, and his eyes water as he strains to breathe.

But still, he instantly recognises the tattoo, goatee and arrogant swagger of the man that leers at him from above.

'Well, well. How're you going, brother?' Merlin chuckles.

'What the hell are you doing?' Dan pants, his face red as he struggles to release the crushing weight.

'Just wanted a chat,' Merlin says, perching on the edge of the bench. 'We haven't seen you for a while. What've you been up to?'

'Laying low.' Dan squeezes the words out in short bursts. 'You know, my little girl.'

'Of course. Baby Ellie. How's she doing? I heard about Stacy. Oh, well, she was a druggo, no great loss. Kid's probably better off without her.'

'What. Do. You. Want?' Dan gasps. Dark dots swim before his eyes.

'I hear you're branching out to human trafficking. Interesting that no one at the club knew about it.' Merlin pulls a knife from his pocket and twirls it between his fingers. 'So why don't you tell me now?'

He moves behind Dan, motioning to his henchmen to return the barbell to its cradle.

Dan coughs and splutters and scrambles to get up, but four enormous, hairy, tattooed arms pin him to the bench.

Merlin positions the dagger at Dan's jugular, sliding it along his throat. Droplets of blood drip down his skin.

'Call me old-fashioned but I admire anyone who has some skill with a blade,' Merlin chuckles as the edge of the knife pushes against Dan's veins. 'I'd kind of like the opportunity to keep my hand in, if you know what I mean.'

'I heard about this opportunity,' Dan croaks. 'Something the club could get in on. Make a motza. But I didn't want to tell the boys until I checked it out.'

'Interesting. And at what point were you going to let the rest of us in on this new business venture?'

'I told you. Once I knew if it was legit. No one's tried this before. Women have been smuggled into Australia as pros but no one's tried to take Aussie women out of the country and sell them. It's groundbreaking.'

'Groundbreaking, hey? Who's running this gig? The Comancheros? Gypsy Jokers? Rebels?'

'I swear to God, I don't know. I heard about it from a buyer. He pointed me to an old fella who wouldn't give me his name. He looks like a pedo. That's who I've been dealing with.'

'What about the cops? They're not totally useless. You can only write off so many missing chicks before it starts to look sus.' Merlin moves the knife up Dan's face and over his left eye.

'The cops know nothin'!' Dan sputters as the knife hovers above his eyeball. 'They're clueless!'

'You wouldn't lie to me, would you, Tiny?'

'No way! Never. I'm telling you the cops are in the dark.'

Dan whimpers as Merlin places the tip of blade against the skin at the edge of his eye, tapping it three times. Then he slides the weapon to his ear, rubbing the soft fleshy lobe with the flat blade before tracing it to Dan's mouth and circling his lips. 'See no evil, hear no … you know the rest, don't you, Tiny? Reckon we should take this conversation somewhere more private.'

He nods to his two enforcers, who drag Dan – thrashing to escape their grip – out the door. Merlin smears the blood from his dagger on Dan's towel before tossing it to a group of men standing by the exit.

'Clean up. No blood. No DNA. No footage. No records. No traces. We were never here.'

Chapter 26

Thick plumes of black smoke rise into the sky, blocking the first rays of dawn. Laura dons a face mask, but the acrid smell of burning debris and smoke still seeps through. A resounding crash booms as the gym roof collapses, gutted by fire then smashed by torrents of water.

From behind the safety barrier, Laura watches Erica gesticulating towards the ruined building and the twisted mess of metal and melted plastic outside it. What was once a black Mustang belonging to her source in the abduction cases. Despite her exasperation, the head of the fire unit stands firm, shaking his head before patting Erica on the shoulder and directing her back to the barrier. Frustrated, Erica stomps back to her small team, leaving the fire chief to handle the media crews waiting for a briefing.

'No good,' Erica says to Laura, Leon and the two officers who were tasked with keeping an eye on Dan. 'It's going to be hours before we can go in.' She rounds on the surveillance team. 'Joel and George, what happened? Why the hell didn't you follow him?'

'I'm sorry, boss,' one of the men says. 'We saw him leave the house, but we lost him in the city. He'd turned off his GPS and phone.'

Erica turns to Leon. 'I need you to check CCTV and get what you can from traffic cameras. We need to find him – and I need to know if he left here alone or with someone else. Voluntarily or otherwise.'

Leon nods, glancing at Laura before climbing into his car and pulling away.

'Laura,' Erica goes on, 'I want you and Ki to come with me to search his place, try and find any clues about where he's gone, or something Ki can use to track him. We already know he's not at any of the safe houses.

'You two,' she growls to Joel and George, who look like guilty schoolboys caught misbehaving in class, 'stay here and call me as soon as we get the green light to go in.'

It takes a while to go over Dan's apartment. Clothes are strewn all over the bedroom, unwashed dishes are piled in the sink, and the kitchen bin is overflowing. The whole place smells like a brewery. The search turns up a small amount of meth and cash hidden inside the bed frame and an empty bag in the wardrobe but nothing to indicate a struggle or that Dan has taken off.

Laura pulls two dirty t-shirts from the floor and places them in front of Ki to get Dan's scent, but the smell of him is everywhere, and it's impossible for Ki to catch a trail.

It's mid-afternoon before Erica gets a call saying it'll be early next morning before they can examine the fire scene and the informant's car. Fire crews and engineers are still making the site safe; it will be cordoned off and they'll have officers stationed at the site protecting the potential crime scene.

'There's nothing more you can do today,' Erica tells Laura. 'Go home and get some rest. They're bringing in a specialist dog trained to detect fuel and liquids used to ignite fires tomorrow, maybe we'll get something then.'

Laura nods. She wants nothing more than to take an early mark and relax at home, run a hot bath and collapse on the couch with Ki. But finding herself alone with Erica as they walk back to their cars, thoughts about Simon and the codes hidden in his cabinet swirl to the front of her mind.

It's now or never.

'So, how did Simon enjoy the night out?' she asks.

'He had a great time,' Erica replies. She smiles, the change of subject from losing her informant seeming to lift her mood. 'We both did. Although we sure felt it the next day.'

'I know what you mean. Leon and I both had cracker hangovers too.' Laura opens the back of the car and waits for Ki to jump into his crate. 'You both seem happy together.'

'To be honest, it all happened very quickly, but it feels right. We're a good match.'

Laura chews at the inside of her lip, and the extended silence cues Erica in that something's wrong. 'What's up? Forget I'm your boss for a moment. I'm your friend. You can talk to me about anything.'

Laura steadies herself, hoping Erica will still feel the same way once she's finished. 'You remember I used to dream about the Shadow Man? Well, he's back in my dreams, tormenting me.'

'Okay.'

'He keeps talking about revenge and taunting me to be careful who I trust. But I've been dreaming about Gran too, like she's trying to reach me, warn me about someone. It's all really muddled and confused. But there was someone else in my last dream too. Simon.'

Erica's face creases into a frown. 'All right. And what was he doing in this dream?'

'He was in the hospital with Gran. She pointed at him, then Gary's voice came out of her, warning me not to trust him.'

'And so now you don't?'

'I thought it was just alcohol and being so tired, but then I…'

'You what?'

Laura's eyes go to the ground, unable to look at her friend. 'I searched his office.'

She looks up to find Erica staring at her in silence. Laura shuffles from foot to foot as she waits for Erica to speak. 'What did you find?'

'He has a key hidden behind his medical certificate. It opens the filing cabinet, which has a false bottom.' The words are tumbling out now. 'He has a folder in there with these strange co-ordinates or codes in it. I didn't want to say anything, but I can't get it out of my head. My dreams have been true before, and if I'd acted on them sooner at Wallaby Rock, maybe we could have stopped Gary before he killed Yvette or Mia. I couldn't bear it if something happened to you, but I was frightened and nervous about saying anything.'

Erica returns to staring at her in silence.

'Please say something,' Laura begs.

'Thank you for telling me, Laura,' Erica responds at last, 'but this time you're wrong.' Her voice is calm but her tone serious, the way she sounds when she's running the team briefings. No emotion. All business. This isn't Erica the Friend speaking. It's her boss. 'Simon helps people every day. He's nothing like Gary. You said yourself you were tired and had a big hangover. I think you were right the first time, that your dream was the byproduct of that. There's nothing to worry about.'

'But what about the folder? What if he's working for someone? He could –'

'He's not up to anything or working for anyone. He's a *doctor*, Laura. I know him. I trust him. He's a good person. Now I appreciate you raising it with me, but let's leave it there.'

'Maybe just check his study …' Laura begins, but Erica's intense glare stops her.

'I said, *leave it,* Laura. I don't want to hear about it again!' Erica takes a deep, calming breath. 'I said there's nothing more you can do today. Take the rest of the day off and I'll see you bright and early tomorrow.'

Laura drags herself through the front door and weighs up going for a run or having a hot shower and curling up in her pyjamas. She feels stretched and wrung out after her conversation with Erica; being honest with her only raised a wall between them, and the idea that their friendship won't recover from it gnaws at her. She hopes Erica's right, that her dream was just a muddled, drunken nightmare, and there's nothing to worry about.

She opts for a run with Ki to clear her head, then treats herself to a bubble bath. Lowering her body into the frothy water, she rests her head against the bath pillow, breathing in the fragrance of coconut and lime from a scented candle. Her phone and a glass of wine are propped up on a bamboo tray spanning the bath, and she clicks on the mix tape playlist Leon made for her. Closing her eyes, she listens to the soothing music before taking a sip of rosé.

The ping of a message interrupts her, and she wipes her hands on a towel before checking her phone. A grin spreads across her face. It's Leon.

HEY, SLACKER. WHERE ARE YOU? I'VE BEEN HERE ALL DAY. YOU TALK TO ERICA? MISS YOU BOTH

Laura sends a photo of the aromatic candle and wine on the bamboo tray, then types a reply.

KI AND I HAD A VERY BUSY DAY ACTUALLY BUT COULDN'T DO ANY MORE SO GOT AN EARLY MARK. YES, TALKED TO ERICA. SHE DOESN'T BELIEVE ME. TOLD ME TO DROP IT. MAYBE SHE'S RIGHT.

Three dots appear on the screen, showing Leon is typing a reply. She sips more wine and the phone pings.

YOU DID THE RIGHT THING. SORRY SHE DIDN'T BELIEVE YOU. MUST BE HARD FOR HER TO THINK SOMEONE SHE LOVES IS ON THE DARK SIDE. GIVE HER TIME.

The dots come up again as he types more.

THE MOST IMPORTANT THING THOUGH …

She waits while he taps in more.

THAT BATH FIT TWO?

The heat rising in Laura's face has nothing to do with the temperature of the water. Last night, they had snuggled and smooched on the couch; she had wanted to keep going, but Leon had been the responsible one, ending the make-out session before it got out of hand. This is an escalation. She replies quickly.

YOU'VE SEEN MY PLACE. IT'S A SHOEBOX. SURE WE COULD SQUEEZE IN AND MAKE IT WORK THOUGH.

The phone pings again.

I'LL TAKE YOU UP ON THAT ANOTHER NIGHT. YOU MUST BE BEAT. KNOW I AM. FEW MORE HOURS HERE THEN EARLY TO BED. MAYBE THIS WEEKEND?

Laura laughs at the pleading-face emoji, pushing away the disappointment of not being with Leon tonight. Sensible, cautious Laura tells her not to rush things, that their relationship is raw and new, but her heart and her body are saying something else. Leon told her he was falling for her; no guy has ever said that to her before. Truth is, she wasn't ready for it and didn't have the guts to tell him the same.

But she is. She's falling hard. All she wants is for him to hold her in his arms and tell her everything between her and Erica will be all right. She fires off a quick reply.

IT'S A DEFINITE POSSIBILITY.

Then hesitates before adding:

I'D LIKE TO TELL MY PARENTS ABOUT US. MAYBE MEET YOUR MUM FIRST? THAT OK? OR TOO SOON?

She flicks bubbles away from her phone and waits nervously for his reply.

I'D LOVE THAT. SHE AND HER BOYFRIEND ARE HERE THIS WEEKEND. SHE'LL BE THRILLED.

Laura places her wine on the tray and ducks her head under the water before emerging and shaking the bubbles from her hair. Half an hour later, she's on the phone to her mother and father, but when she tells them she's dating a new guy, their surprise is a little forced.

Bloody Sarah!

Chapter 27

Simon's car is in the driveway, and the lights are on when Erica arrives home that evening. She's still chewing over the day's events. Back at the office, she and Detective Jeffries had met with Assistant Commissioner Stirling and engaged in a heated debate about whether to keep monitoring Cain Anderson or issue a search and arrest warrant, and raid Cain Anderson's house now. They decided to keep watching him – they still don't have the information they need for the auction, and with Dan missing, the ageing criminal is now their only link to the big players.

Some of her dark mood dissipates, however, the second she unlocks the front door and his deep voice greets her.

'Hey, you're just in time for dinner. I've made spinach and ricotta cannelloni and there's a glass of cab sav with your name on it.'

Erica smiles to herself. Simon's just finished a long shift himself but still managed to cook one of her favourites.

Laura was wrong. He's no Gary.

Dropping her bag in their bedroom, she calls out, 'I'll be there in a minute,' before taking the pins out of her bun and letting her hair fall in loose waves around her shoulders. Then she takes off her work gear and slips into a satin nightie and dressing gown.

As she pads up the hallway, she stops outside Simon's study. The sound of the evening news bulletin echoes from the lounge room, and she peers down the hallway to the kitchen. No sign of Simon. He must be on the couch.

What the hell are you thinking, Erica?

She turns the knob and eases the study door open. She glances around the room. There's a key in the filing cabinet, the one where Laura said Simon keeps his secrets locked away. Erica crosses the room, turns the key and unlocks the drawers. Quietly, she pulls them open and examines the back of the cabinet.

No false floor, no file with codes or coordinates, just Simon's notebooks and papers. She flicks through a couple and finds nothing but details of medical cases, treatment options and outcomes.

She closes and locks the cabinet, then turns to the bookshelf and picks up the frame holding Simon's degree. She turns it over, her fingers probing for the velvet pouch. There isn't one.

Laura must have dreamt all of it.

Erica lets out a long breath, almost ashamed of the relief washing over her.

'Honey, your dinner's getting cold.'

Jumping, she turns to find Simon leaning in the doorway, grinning at her. 'Sorry, I didn't mean to scare you.'

'That's okay, I didn't hear you. Being on edge is an occupational hazard. I noticed the light on and thought you were in here working. Then I got distracted looking at your frame. I never realised how lovely it is before.'

'Not as lovely as you.'

'Hold that thought,' Erica says, replacing the frame on the shelf and walking into his arms.

At 6:30 the next morning, Erica meets the forensics team at the burned-out gym. She's never been part of a fire investigation before and observes the light-hearted banter between the two forensic officers and the chief fire investigator – all three kitted out in overalls, masks and gloves – with detached amusement. The tone changes when they notice her, however, and the chief, a bespectacled, balding man in his mid-forties, slips back into his official persona. He shakes hands with her, before issuing brief instructions in a tone that leaves no room for argument.

'There's gear over there – put some on and follow us in. Don't touch anything.'

Once she's clad in protective clothing, the team gets down to work. When the specialist detection dog arrives – a black Labrador named Jet – Erica trails behind as the team pick their way through the blackened rubble.

Several times, the dog stops and indicates a find to its handler. The chief fire investigator tapes off those areas before photos are taken and samples collected. It's time-consuming and painstaking work, and it's lunchtime before they call a halt to their examination of the gym and the car outside.

She waits for her opportunity to catch the chief on his own, then takes him to one side.

'So, what's the verdict?' she asks. It's pretty plain the fire was deliberate – how else would it take out the car as well as the building? – but she's hoping for something, anything else that would count as a lead.

The chief gives her the flat look of a man who's investigated over 50 fires in his career and had to answer the same question at all of them. 'We have to wait for lab results to be one hundred per cent sure, but the speed and ferocity of the fire, in both the gym and the car outside, together with the detections by the dog team, indicate the use of accelerant and lots of it. Whoever did this wanted to be one hundred per cent sure they left no trace they were in there.' He claps her on the shoulder. 'So good luck finding out who it was.'

Chapter 28

Laura stops when she registers the name on the office door. Spinning on her heels, she marches, Ki by her side, to Erica's office and knocks twice. There's no response, so she turns the handle. Locked. Fuming, she returns to the foyer, collecting her phone from her locker before dialling Erica's number.

'You gave Alex my office,' she says as soon as Erica picks up. Red blotches of anger are creeping up her neck.

'Good morning to you, too,' Erica replies. 'And yes, I did. That office was assigned to a detective. You got to use it for a while until we found one.'

'It would have been nice to know before I came in,' Laura says, her face now beetroot red. 'Does this have anything to do with what happened yesterday?'

Erica sighs loudly, and Laura pictures her raising her eyebrows the way she does when someone says something she considers pointless. 'No. Of course not. Look, I'm sorry I didn't message you, but I've been busy at the fire scene. I've organised a desk for you alongside Leon and his team. I assumed you wouldn't mind sitting there.'

'Right. Thanks. It's just … are we okay?'

Erica's voice rises enough that Laura pulls the phone from her ear. 'We are if you drop it. I told you, there's nothing to worry about. Trust me.'

Before Laura can even contemplate responding, the line goes dead.

A small box holding her meagre personal belongings and notebooks sits on the desk next to Matt when she and Ki arrive at their new digs. There's a pink Post-it note stuck to the top of it: *I have news. Come and see me as soon as you get in. Alex*

'Is everything okay?' Leon whispers over from behind her.

'Yep. It's fine. Detective Jeffries is using the office, so now you have the pleasure of my company,' Laura says. Tears threaten to bubble to the surface but she pushes them down.

'Would you like to go for a walk?'

'Later,' Laura replies, waving the note in front of him. 'I've been summoned.'

Leon rubs her shoulder, then retreats to his desk, giving her space to compose herself as she unpacks her things. When the box is empty, she grabs her notebook and pen, and with Ki in tow, returns to what was once her office. She raps on the door and, without waiting for a reply, pushes it open.

'Ah, good, you're finally in,' Alex says.

Laura bites back a sarcastic reply and instead pulls up a chair. Ki lies on the floor beside her, his head on his paws, and closes his eyes.

'I have some initial data from Adam, our financial analyst,' Alex says as she hands a paper over the desk to Laura. 'It's an interesting read. There are some complex financial arrangements that are taking time to unpack, but the monetary injection the Larsons received, the one that saved them from bankruptcy, wasn't solely due to an extension of their loan.'

Laura glances up from the report. 'What do you mean? Who else is funding them?'

'That's the question I want answered,' Alex replies, grinning at her. 'The Larsons were in more debt than they let on. The extra loan would've only kept them afloat for another six months. Instead, they received a substantial windfall from a mystery company based in Manila.'

'How much did they get?'

'More than half a million.'

Laura's eyes widen. 'That is substantial. Do we know who owns the company? Do they have any connections to the Australian mafia?'

Alex's smile widens. 'I said you have good instincts. I'm still digging into that, but I'd bet we'll find one. Now, tell me how you went? Did you find anything leading to our missing informant?'

'Nothing. No physical clues, and the guy's scent was too widespread and dense for Ki to track anything. Got to say, this informant? Doesn't look good for him.'

'He could've set this up himself,' Alex suggests. 'Erica said he was getting cold feet. He might have decided to fake his abduction or death. No one looks for a dead man.'

Laura digests the possibility for a moment. 'Do you think he would do that? Erica said he was desperate for witness protection, for him and his family. Surely he wouldn't risk leaving them unprotected?'

Alex shrugs. 'It's just a theory. But after more than 10 years as a detective, I never rule anything out. Anyway, back to today's business. I've spoken to our analyst, Adam, and asked him to also get cracking on all the businesses where the missing women worked,' Alex says. 'But I have a special job for you. You've got that country girl charm going on; I'd like you to use it and get chummy with the people at Armidale station. Line up a visit.'

'Of course,' Laura says, ignoring the backhanded compliment. She rises from her chair, and Ki jumps to his feet.

'By the way,' Alex says with a smirk as Laura heads out. 'Sorry to kick you out of the office, but from what I hear, you'll be much happier in your new spot.'

Back at her new desk, Laura catches Leon's eye, motioning to Ki and then the exit. He nods and gets up to follow them. Laura notices Matt nudge Jess, and the two glance at each other, sniggering, before returning to their work.

'Does everybody know about us?' she asks Leon once they're alone. 'Alex gave me this evil grin when she said I'd be happier at my new desk. She's so bloody smug. I can't stand it.'

Leon's laugh is loud enough to bounce off the walls of the lift. 'We work with people employed for their keen observation skills. I'd be disappointed if they hadn't worked it out. We go for coffee and a walk together every day – sometimes twice a day. Everyone has noticed the spark between us.' He grins. 'But on the upside, we don't have to hide that we're dating anymore.'

'I know,' Laura says, ruffling Ki's fur. 'But I still don't like other people sticking their noses into my business.'

'Never mind that,' Leon says as they exit the lift car and head towards the park. 'I spoke to Mum and she's really excited to meet you. She's invited us for lunch on Saturday – her famous fish curry.'

'I spoke to my parents too,' Laura says. 'They're keen to meet you as well, but we'll need to coordinate time off so we can spend a few days with them. It's a long way to go for a quick visit.' As soon as they are clear of the building, she slips her hand into his.

Leon rubs his thumb on the inside of her palm and moves closer so their arms touch as they walk.

They sit at their usual bench under their gum tree and Laura rests her hand on top of his. The touch of his skin sets her pulse racing, and she wonders if he can hear her heart pounding. *Sensible Laura be damned.*

'Now that our relationship is out in the open and our parents know about us, maybe we don't have to wait until the weekend to spend time together,' she suggests. 'Perhaps you can come over this evening for dinner? You've already figured out that I'm a rubbish cook, but I'm a whizz at ordering in.'

Leon turns his face to hers, and she holds her breath, gazing into his eyes, waiting for his reply. Except the creases around his eyes deepen and her confidence falters.

'Are you sure?' he says, reading between the lines. 'I don't want to push you.'

'I'm sure. I don't want to wait. Come over tonight. Maybe bring your toothbrush?' she adds, putting the offer out in the open.

'Do you know how much I want to kiss you right now?' Leon whispers … only for Ki to push his head into Laura's hand.

'Hey, boy, sorry,' she says. 'I haven't forgotten. Let's do that walk.'

And kiss or no kiss, all thought of Simon, Erica and even her old office disappears for a while.

When she returns to the office, Laura calls the officer in charge at Armidale, Senior Sergeant Amy Fuller, only to be told she is at a community event with the mayor. Opting to put her time to good use while she waits for a call back, Laura begins searching recent

162

cases of serious criminal activity around Armidale. She saves extracts of reports and media articles to a folder on her computer before cross-referencing the publicly available information against police records, and by lunchtime, she has enough material to kickstart her conversation with Fuller.

She glances at Leon; he has his headphones on and is engrossed in something on his screen. Laura mulls over what he said earlier: that he'd be surprised if their colleagues hadn't figured out they were dating. It's time to make things official. Accessing the intranet, she finds the form for change of circumstances, fills it out with details of her relationship with Leon, and sends it to HR.

Emailing the form makes it real, and she can't help but grin as she recalls the text messages they shared about her bath, and what she hopes will happen next.

Get a grip. You've got work to do.

As if to drive the thought home, a message pops up on her screen. It's from Erica. She wants to see Laura. Urgently.

The distinctive smell of smoke from the fire scene that cakes Erica's clothes and hair wafts into the corridor as the boss waves her and Ki in.

'Another woman has gone missing,' Erica says. 'Up in Katoomba in the Blue Mountains. She went for a hike this morning but hasn't returned. She isn't answering her phone, coverage is patchy, and GPS is inactive. Search and rescue are heading there now, but after your success at the Games, you're in hot demand. The DC wants you and Ki to help, but you need to leave now.'

Laura nods, excited to be on the frontline of a search. But then she thinks about what she'll be leaving behind – not just that she'll have to postpone her plans with Leon, but that she doesn't want to leave the team in a lurch, or her friendship with Erica up in the air. 'Will you be okay?' she asks, choosing her words with care. She wants to make amends before she leaves, not make things worse. 'A lot is going on with the informant, fire and investigating the businesses.'

'We'll manage,' Erica says. She sounds tired but not upset. 'Alex is all over it. You'd better get going.'

Back at her new desk, Laura finds Matt sitting at Leon's workstation. He looks up at her and Ki and smiles. 'Oh, hey. Leon and Jess are at a meeting. I'm holding the fort. Leaving him a phone message,' he says, grabbing a note and waving it in his hand.

'I was hoping to catch him myself,' she says. 'We've been ordered to an urgent search in the Blue Mountains, got to leave right now.'

'Post-it?' Matt asks, offering her the pad.

'It's okay, I'll text him.'

She collects her phone from her locker, and as they rush to the car, she punches out a message to Leon, explaining what's happened and how they'll have to reschedule their plans.

His reply is brief.

Chapter 29

The late-afternoon sun shimmers through the tree canopy as Laura parks behind a squad of police, fire and SES vehicles. As soon as she exits the car, she is assaulted by the cold mountain air and quickly dons a thick jacket before releasing Ki from his crate in the back.

A tall woman with a blonde pixie haircut is pacing outside a marquee erected for the search operation, chewing her fingernails. As soon as Ki jumps to the ground, she rushes over and grabbing Laura's arm, pants, 'Have you found her?'

'I'm sorry, we've just arrived. You should talk to the head of the search operation.'

'No one's telling me anything,' the woman says, digging her fingers deeper into Laura's sleeve. As she disengages from the woman's grip, Laura notices a delicate tattoo of a swallow on the side of the woman's neck.

'Cate can't just disappear,' the woman goes on. 'Something must've happened to her. She might be injured. Bitten by a snake. Fallen down a cliff. Please, you have to find her.'

'I understand, but you have to let us do our job,' Laura says. 'Sorry, but if you'll excuse us …'

Breaking away, she heads to the tent and checks in. She pours herself a coffee from the urn and devours a sandwich while she waits for further instructions, and soon she and Ki are joined by a large golden Labrador and her handler.

'Hi, I'm Jacob,' the handler says as the police dogs sniff and greet each other. 'And this is Cleo.'

'Laura, and Ki,' she replies. 'Up from –'

'Oh, I know who you are,' Jacob says, grinning broadly. 'Gold medallists at the games and all. We've come in from Dubbo.'

'If I could have your attention, please.' The local SES chief and head of Police Search and Rescue have moved into position by a briefing board set up at the rear of the tent, and as they begin to speak, the assembled search team falls silent.

'We're here to find Cate Bell,' the head of Search and Rescue begins, indicating a picture of the missing woman on the board; she is tall, athletic and has a raven bob and startling green eyes. Laura makes out a swallow tattoo on her left shoulder that matches the one on the woman outside.

'Cate is 22 and is here on holiday with her girlfriend Anna. She left their bed and breakfast early this morning to take photos and hike the trails. Cate is a budding photographer and was keen to explore the mountains.

'Cate was last sighted picking up a coffee and toasted sandwich from a café near the B&B around 8 am. She then started walking toward the Three Sisters to take photos of the views, telling her partner she wouldn't be long. Unfortunately, she hadn't returned by midday, and there's been no response to multiple calls and messages from her partner. It was at this point that the police were notified and search and rescue efforts commenced.'

Laura pays close attention as the SES chief talks the search parties through several maps of the area and allocates teams to cover the ground. She and Jacob are handed clothing that belongs to the missing woman and take turns holding the material in front of their dogs' noses before wishing each other good luck and splitting up to join their respective search teams.

They don't get long to search – a little more than three hours pass before the sun starts to set and the temperature plunges. Beautiful as the rugged bushland is – framed by towering sandstone cliffs, the region is famous around Australia and the world – the tracks that wind through the mountains are steep and slippery, and no place to be wandering around in fading light.

As the last few calls of 'Cate' echo through the scrub, the search is halted for the night, to recommence at dawn. And returning to the SES operations area, Laura can't help but worry if the young woman can possibly survive out there until then.

After a good night's sleep at a pet-friendly motel, Laura and Ki rejoin their search team for the morning briefing. Frost blankets the ground, and the cold eats into Laura's bones as she blows on her hands, her gloves doing little to keep her fingers warm. She wonders again how Cate could possibly have survived the night, exposed to the harsh elements, and it's clear she's not the only one thinking that. There's a frantic and nervous energy amongst the group now. No one wants the young woman to spend another night in the open.

Guzzling down hot brews, the teams set off again. It's a long slog, and the chatter amongst the searchers dies down as the day stretches on. Ki sniffs diligently along and around the tracks, but hours pass and there's no sign of Cate. Then, just as Laura's hopes are fading, the radios carried by the search teams crackle and burst to life with cheers and messages of relief.

Cate has been found.

Laura pieces the story together from the radio reports as she heads back to base. Cate had left the main trail to cut through the heavy bush, hoping to capture a different angle and perspective of the Three Sisters for her Instagram account. As she was leaning over the edge, the ground gave way under her feet and she slid 200 metres to a narrow ledge below. Her phone and camera were smashed into tiny pieces; knocked unconscious, she didn't hear rescuers calling for her.

In the end, it was Jacob and Cleo who discovered her clinging to the side of a cliff with a broken leg, suffering a heavy concussion and hypothermia.

As Laura, Ki and their team approach camp, the whirring of a helicopter shakes the trees, and they pause to watch the chopper fly overhead, cheering as it zooms to Cate's rescue. But as she waves to the helicopter passing above, Laura notices that Ki's attention is elsewhere.

Nose to the ground, the dog sniffs left, then right, then left again … then races off the trail and into the trees.

'Ki!' Laura calls out before giving chase, several of the search team crashing through the bush close behind her. Ki pivots and takes a sharp, right-angle turn. Laura, unable to halt her momentum so quickly, almost collides with a tall stringybark gum. She resumes her pursuit and finds Ki pawing at the roots of another tree.

'Ki, stop!' Laura commands, and her canine partner obeys immediately, sitting and cocking his head to one side, waiting for his reward.

He's found something. Laura just can't imagine what.

The rest of the team gather around to inspect Ki's discovery, as, kneeling by the tree, Laura gently shifts small mounds of dirt and leaves.

Slowly, the side profile of a face appears.

Laura gasps loudly, rocks backwards in shock. Deep cuts that resemble stitches criss-cross the cheek of the face, half buried in the ground, and cameras are already clicking to record the find as Laura backs away.

They'll need to get a forensic team up here to continue the delicate excavation, but even with the eyes and ears of the man removed, Laura has seen enough to recognise him.

Remembering the scent he was exposed to back at the flat, Ki has done his job. He's found their informant. Dan Garfield.

Chapter 30

Assistant Commissioner Stirling, Erica is informed, is at a joint operation briefing with the Australian Federal Police in Canberra and cannot be disturbed. Frustrated, Erica sends him a text instead, telling him there's been a serious new development and she will update him as soon as he's free, then calls Deputy Commissioner Robyn Jones.

The DC, apparently, is also busy, but Erica insists on staying on the line.

'This is a top priority, it cannot wait,' she explains to Jones's assistant.

'I'll have to put you on hold,' the assistant responds, and instantly Erica's ear is filled with infuriatingly monotonous lift music. Erica bites back the swearword she wants to utter, which is just as well, as a moment later Robyn Jones comes on the line.

'Erica. What's so important that it can't wait?'

'I need to talk to you face-to-face. It's not good news.'

'All right. Get up here now. I can give you five minutes, no more. I'm due in a meeting with the Minister.'

Erica breathes in the masculine scent of polished wood and leather as she strides down the executive corridor. The eyes of previous NSW police commissioners and ministers look down at her from the large, framed portraits that line the walls on both sides.

Up ahead, the DC's assistant emerges from Robyn Jones' office, and beckons to Erica to come straight in.

Jones is sitting on a small lounge in the corner, a cup of coffee on the low table in front of her. She waves for Erica to join her, but Erica chooses to stay standing, pacing the floor. She's too wound up to remain still.

'What's so sensitive that you couldn't tell me over the phone?' DC Jones asks.

'We found our source,' Erica explains. 'Dead. His head was discovered earlier today in the Blue Mountains. Senior Constable Murray and PD Ki uncovered it while searching for a missing woman.'

'Christ! What about the rest of the body?'

'No sign. Forensics have removed the head from the scene and are still searching, but that's not the only part of him missing.'

'Go on,' Jones says, her face serious.

'He's missing eyes, ears and a tongue. It reeks of a gangland execution.'

'Correct me if I'm wrong, but the identity of your informant was closely protected.'

'That is correct.'

Jones blows out her cheeks. 'In which case we have a serious problem. Someone is leaking information to the other side. What did Murray tell the search team?'

'Nothing. She called me first and I ordered her not to tell anyone who the head belongs to, including other police officers. I asked her to stay up there a little while and keep her ear to the ground too, monitor for any news leaks.'

'Good. I want this information contained. Restricted to you, me, Murray, Stirling and Professional Standards – I'll notify them myself to start looking for our leak. No one else is to know. This is now a top-secret, high-priority gangland investigation that we cannot discuss with anyone. If someone does, they'll pay for it.'

'Understood, ma'am.'

'Reinforce to Murray that she cannot tell anyone that our source – or part of him – has been found. Everyone must believe he's still missing. I'll call search and rescue and the state SES Director. Tell them this is locked down, a blackout. No one is to speak of it, especially not to the media.'

'What about the informant's mother and child? They may be in danger, and I gave him my word that nothing would happen to them.'

'You shouldn't have done that,' Jones says, scowling. 'We can't guarantee their safety until they're in protection.'

Erica stops pacing and plants her hands on her hips. 'I'm sorry, ma'am, but that baby is now an orphan and her life is possibly in danger. We can't sit back and do nothing!'

Immediately Erica knows she's over-stepped, talking that way to a senior officer, but instead of reprimanding her, the DC simply stands and grips her by the shoulders. 'Yes, we can, and yes, we will. Our priority is identifying our leak or it will compromise *everything*. If we can't, we'll have to shut down the taskforce. So, I need you need to stay focused. Find out who organised the hit and who our mole is.'

'I'll take a wild stab in the dark that Anderson and the Scorpions are involved.'

'Then go get me the evidence to prove it.'

Chapter 31

Even before Merlin and his clubmen turned up at the gym, Dan was worried his time was up.

Now, waking naked and shivering and lashed to a wooden bed frame in a tiny tin shed with no windows, he knows it is.

'Wakey, wakey, sleepyhead,' Merlin mocks as he moves out of the darkness and into the light of a single bulb hanging from the ceiling. He drags a milk crate behind him and drops onto it, sitting by the side of the bed. Reaching out, he touches the blood caking the side of Dan's head; his fingers come away sticky, and he licks them clean.

'They gave you a good knock, hey *brother*. You've been out for hours but that's all right. We've got plenty of time to catch up.' Pulling the dagger from the inside of his jacket, he twirls it between his fingers.

'Tell me, have you ever heard of *lingchi*?'

Dan doesn't respond

'Reckoned not. You don't look like the classically educated type to me. You wouldn't guess, but I went to a ritzy boys' school. My oldies were loaded, lived in a big house on the harbour, all respected and envied.' He chuckles. 'Total lie, though. My old man was a big-name stockbroker with some shonky clients and a wandering eye; couldn't keep it in his pants. Mum coped by knocking herself out with booze and prescription meds. When I arrived, they shunted me off to boarding school.'

He looks down at Dan. 'Hey, not boring you, am I? It's not often I get to talk about the old days. No? I'll go on then.

'So, I topped the class in maths and economics, always had a knack for numbers, but never got the chance to make something of it. There was this teacher who picked on the kids whose families didn't give a shit. The ones no one would care about. Bastard abused me for six years. Six years! I told my parents, but they didn't believe me. You know what turned it all around for me?'

Dan shakes his head.

'Getting out of school and joining the Scorpions. Finally had a real family then. Brothers who'd die for me and I for them. This tatt,' Merlin points to the phoenix wrapped around his neck, 'is to remind me you can rise from the ashes and start again. But things are changin', aren't they? Your generation, you Nikie Bikies, are only in it for yourselves. Posting shit all over social media and thinking the cops won't find out? Jesus, how dumb can you be? And then you think you can swap from one club to another, or even snitch and get away with it. But loyalty … that still means something to me.

'Anyway, getting a little sidetracked here. Where were we? Oh yeah, *lingchi*. It's an ancient form of torture and execution that was used in China for hundreds of years. You might know it as "death by a thousand cuts". It was a punishment used on the worst of traitors. They'd cut bits of your body off over several days. Fingers, toes, knees,' Merlin rubs the blade across the skin between Dan's legs, 'genitals, until finally the person died.'

Dan wills himself not to flinch.

'So that teacher I was telling you about. Mr Mathers. You know he lay on this same bed, in this same shed, right where you are now. I really took my time with him. Took out his tongue first so he couldn't scream, and left his eyes last, so he could watch me work. He lasted four days.' Merlin's voice drifts away, almost wistful as he remembers. 'Listen to me, getting all misty-eyed. Must be old age.'

Merlin shuffles closer to the bed and digs the knife into Dan's pinky, wiggling it back and forth. Dan stifles a cry.

'It's time to 'fess up. Which little piggy you been talking to, eh? It's only a matter of time before I find out. You know I will.' Merlin says, and from the corner of his eye, Dan watches as a wicked grin stretches across Merlin's face. It makes his bikie brother look like a demented clown. 'But by all means, try to hold out if you like.'

Dan loses track of how long it takes, how many days he's spent as Merlin's plaything. He can't even remember which bits have been sliced off. He's tried to stay strong, buying as much time as he can for Ellie and his mum.

He doesn't scream or utter a word. Every time he loses consciousness, Merlin throws icy water on his face and slaps him around until he's ready to start again.

At last, Merlin reappears and reads out loud the messages Dan and Martin shared. 'Got a snitch of my own now,' he says, laughing. 'Got me these little chats of yours. Can you even imagine the kind of chaos I'll be able to cause with someone on the inside?'

It's this that finally breaks Dan.

'Please …' he groans. 'Don't hurt my family. Only … only did what I did for them. Give them … better life.'

Merlin pats him on the cheek. 'I get it, mate. Wish someone had looked out for me like that when I was a kid. I swear your baby girl won't be touched. So … how about we wrap this up, eh?'

Merlin slices out his tongue, takes his ears and removes his eyes. Before he cuts Dan's throat, he tells him he'll leave his head where the cops are sure to find it. 'Need to send a message, don't I?'

As the swift, deep cut to his jugular ends his pain, Dan's last thought is of Ellie.

Chapter 32

The growling in the depths of his stomach tells Leon he needs a break and something to eat.

He and his team have been at it for two days, finding potential routes their informant may have taken, identifying CCTV and traffic cameras along the way, and then requesting access to footage from the night he disappeared. It's a constant stream of vision from different sources, and they've begun the long process of sifting hours and hours of video.

Picking up his phone, he takes pizza orders from the team and calls them in, then he messages Laura as he waits in the foyer for the food. There's no response, but he's not surprised – she's busy on a search. That said, he can't wait for her to get back.

Even before she asked him to stay over, he'd been planning the perfect romantic evening. His ideas involve a bottle of Moët and Chandon, chocolate-dipped strawberries, candles and testing out that bath. Since Laura told him about her experience with Gary, it's become more important for Leon to take it slow and let her set the pace. Luckily, she's made it clear she wants to progress their relationship.

He whistles to himself as he visualises the night he hopes they'll soon enjoy together, and he's cheerful enough to crack jokes as he doles out slices of pizza to Matt and Jess. His good mood lasts until he resumes the tedious job of downloading and distributing footage to himself and his team. Unable to put it off any longer, they don headphones and get to work, scanning, pausing and looking at different angles.

Two hours later, Jess calls Leon and Matt over.

'I've found the black Mustang,' she says. 'Picked it up from a traffic camera as it swung onto Parramatta Road. It disappears down a side lane and I lose it again, but I did spot another vehicle trailing it.'

'One of ours?' Matt asks.

Jess shakes her head and slurps from her drink before responding. 'No, I already checked. At first, I thought it was nothing, but then I thought for that time of the morning, it's odd it takes the same route.'

'Play it for me,' Leon says. She cues up the footage, and they watch as the Mustang speeds along the main road before swerving across two lanes and driving down a back alley. Jess's fingers hover over the button to pause the recording. 'There it is,' she says. The freeze frame shows a white van, and she advances the footage so they can watch it swing across the road and hurtle down the same narrow lane as the Mustang.

'Did you get the plate?' Leon asks.

'I already took a screenshot. I'm sending it to you now.'

'Good job. Keep at it.' Leon heads back to his workstation and immediately sends the number plate to Erica.

They soon learn the plates are fake, cloned from a stolen car. They review the van from different angles and try to enhance the faces inside, but the windows are heavily tinted, and all they can decipher is a shadowy outline of a driver and passenger. Both have their faces covered with masks, still a common practice after COVID.

Matt disappears for half an hour to do a coffee run, but by the time he returns, Leon has decided they're not getting anywhere. He's about to send the team home, when Jess calls him over once more.

'I picked them both up again,' she says. 'The Mustang drives down the road leading to the gym before the camera angle runs out. The van follows and pulls up outside a tobacconist, but all I get is the edge of the front bonnet. It hangs around for around five minutes before continuing, then I lose that too.'

Jess saves the clip and sends it to Leon, who forwards it to Erica, before going to her office to talk her through it. 'We've not been able to find any other known CCTV cameras in the street,' he tells her. 'We'll have to move on to checking security cameras of businesses near the gym.'

'Excellent work, Leon,' Erica says. 'And thank the team too. You guys stand down; you've worked your butts off. Go home and get some rest. I'll want you all refreshed and ready to go in the morning.'

'Thanks, boss.'

'Okay, everyone, we're out of here,' Leon announces when he returns. 'Boss's orders.'

'Excellent,' Matt says, stretching and rubbing his eyes, and within minutes all three are waiting for the lift to the ground floor.

But as the elevator doors slide open, Leon slaps his hand to his forehead.

'Damn. I forgot to lock up. I don't want to get a breach. You guys go on, no need to hang about for me. See you tomorrow.'

He waits until the doors close and the lift is descending before heading back to the office.

Chapter 33

The phone vibrates across the glass coffee table, and Cain rushes from the kitchen to snatch it up before it falls onto the hard timber floor. As soon as he hits the green button, a familiar, raspy voice says, 'You were right. It's done. You owe me.'

His mouth hangs open, and he holds the phone to his ear long after the click of the call disconnecting, the reality of what he's heard slowly sinking in. When he does, at last, swear loudly, the word that erupts from his mouth sounds like a crow cawing.

He shuffles to a dark cedar cabinet in the corner and digs out a bottle of Scotch and a glass tumbler. Hands trembling, he pours a full shot before throwing his head back and swallowing. He refills the glass and repeats the action. By the third shot, there's only a slight tremor when he raises the tumbler to his lips.

He knew it. Deep in his guts he had felt something was off about Tiny. If only he'd never responded to the man's first messages, taken more time to check him out before telling him about their business.

If only.

Now he's exposed. But as he rehashes his conversations with the big man, his heart rate slows. He's confident he didn't give the snitch anything that would lead the police to his boss. The problem now is that he has a debt to pay. That won't go down well. Not one *tiny* bit.

Time to get it over with.

He opens a hidden drawer in the cabinet and removes a phone and SIM cards. He only uses this device for *TITAN* communication, and once he has it set up, he calls his boss.

'The new buyer talked. But now he's lost his voice.'

'What the fuck? What're you doing? Putting out ads? Didn't you check him? What did he know?'

'He had credentials, but he squealed. I didn't give him *TITAN* access or details about the auction, and he never found out who's in charge.'

'Good.'

'Thing is the friend I had take care of it? He wants a piece of the pie.'

'Then that *piece* is coming out of your cut. Meantime, we have to move. Fast. They'll have eyes and ears on you. I'll deal with that. Deep clean and don't stuff it up. There can be no traces. Wait for instructions and be ready.'

Cain gets started at once. Donning gloves, protective glasses and a mask, he pours high-grade hospital bleach into a bucket and begins the meticulous task of wiping down all surfaces and the wooden floor, paying close attention to bathrooms, toilets and the kitchen.

He moves on to the bedroom. Flicking on the lamp in the corner, his eyes drawn to the ornate iron bed and its bare, queen-size mattress. His place was only a stopover before the women were moved to new locations where they were prepared for their new lives, but while they were here … His pulse quickens as he remembers the fear in the women's eyes, the bodies he's touched and the delightful moments he's captured. He'd been onto a good thing.

Until Tiny.

Anger surges through him at the betrayal. He hopes Merlin made it slow and painful. No one should snitch and get away with it.

His phone pings, and he reads his new instructions. He has to hurry. They won't wait forever. He finishes the sanitisation of the mattress, bedframe and all remaining furniture. Taking the rug from the bedroom floor, he grunts with the effort of squishing it into a large garbage bag, then does the same for the pillows, sheets and linen stacked in the cupboard.

After six hours of continuous cleaning, he leans, exhausted, on his suitcase by the back door, the garbage bags ready for collection and disposal. His *TITAN* phone pings with a new message:

PATH CLEAR. GO.

186

Chapter 34

Juggling a hot coffee and her laptop, Erica rushes to answer the phone. It's her boss, his voice coming in short, clipped bursts, like gunfire.

'Martin. We need to talk. In person. In the DC's office. Get up here. Now.'

'On my way, sir.' She hangs up, backing out the door and locking it behind her.

Stirling is waiting outside the DC's office and waves her inside, where, as well as DC Jones, there's a middle-aged, bespectacled and greying man in a spotless uniform. She doesn't recognise him, but from his general bearing and attitude, she has a pretty good idea who he is.

'Leading Senior Constable,' Stirling says, 'This is Assistant Commissioner Jeff Nunn. Head of the Professional Standards Unit.'

Bingo, she thinks before swapping her coffee cup to her other hand and shaking Nunn's. 'Morning, sir.'

'Please, sit,' the DC says, indicating the couch as she pulls up a plush armchair. 'Right. Let's get to it. Jeff's team has uncovered something important. Jeff?'

'Thank you, Ma'am,' Nunn says. 'We've started investigating the taskforce and anyone aware of the work you are doing, paying particular attention to anyone who has had contact with or knowledge of your source.' Erica nods. 'More than 20 people are either working on or supporting the taskforce, but of those, only a handful knew about your informant. The DC and you, six surveillance officers, Senior Constable Murray, Detective Jeffries, three staff from the technical team, and the head of Cyber.

'Of those, only two people had ongoing, direct contact with your source. You and the head of the technical team, Leon Campbell. How well do you know him?'

Erica plants her coffee cup on the table. 'He's been with the taskforce from the start,' she says, hoping the warmth of her tone conveys her belief in Leon's good character. 'And he's been working on the tech side for several years. His father was a well-respected officer who died on the job a few years ago. Lives at home, helping his mum. He's a good guy.'

'Did you know he's dating Senior Constable Murray?'

'I did. Laura – Senior Constable Murray – talked to me about it. I told her she needed to declare their relationship; make sure it was on the record.'

'She did. Leon Campbell didn't.'

'Well, maybe he hasn't gotten to it yet. They haven't been dating that long and we've been busy, you know.' Erica can't help the push-back, the sarcasm in her voice.

'Of course, Leading Senior Constable. But as you're aware, there are processes that need to be followed. Not doing so shows Campbell is comfortable operating outside the rules.'

'That doesn't mean he's the mole.'

'Erica, please,' the DC says. 'Let him continue.'

'In his role, Leon Campbell leads a team of two junior staff,' Nunn goes on. 'They're responsible for looking after and monitoring cameras and listening devices, as well as sourcing and reviewing footage and images that may be relevant to the taskforce. Our initial review suggests there's some missing material.'

'What do you mean, missing material?' Erica asks.

'The night your source disappeared, he was observed and later tracked travelling in his vehicle toward a gym in the early hours of the morning, where his car was later found, burned out. Mr Campbell and his team identified a white van tailing the source. The plates were fake, and they were unable to get sufficient visual identification of the driver and passenger. The last sighting of the van and the source's vehicle was outside a business on the road leading to the gym before the camera reached its limit.

'Except there's another camera, on the wall of a nearby tobacconist, facing the gym. The same business that the van was parked beside. A business that we suspect has connections to the Scorpions. Leon Campbell never informed you or anyone else of the camera's existence.'

'Hold on,' Erica cuts in. 'Leon and his team worked for two days straight on that job. They might have missed it. They were exhausted, so I sent them home to get some rest.'

'We know,' Nunn replies. 'But Mr Campbell returned to his desk after the others left, and the cameras inside the taskforce offices show he didn't leave the office for another 45 minutes. Why? What was he doing for that long? We believe he knew there was more material and stayed back, accessed the other footage and deleted it. Footage that may have shown who was hunting your source.'

'Can you prove it?' the DC asks.

Jeff turns to address the senior officer. 'Not yet, Ma'am, but —'

'I still can't believe Leon would do this,' Erica cuts in, 'but perhaps there's a way to find out for sure.' She turns to Nunn. 'You said your review has only scratched the surface, but you've uncovered this discrepancy. You have the power and access to keep monitoring Leon and his team, in secret and without detection. Why don't you keep doing that? Then we can know for sure if he's the mole.'

The Professional Standards officer faces the DC, ignores Erica's suggestion. 'My recommendation is that we question Mr Campbell and review all his activities and devices. You may want to consider suspending him pending a full and proper investigation. If he's exonerated, he can return to work, no harm done. If not, well, we'll get to that later.'

'What if it's not him!' Erica barks. 'Then his reputation is trashed and we are none the wiser about who's leaking intel. A full investigation will take months! In the meantime, the taskforce falters and more women could be placed in danger.'

'Deputy Commissioner,' Nunn says, his voice flat and calm, 'I must insist on following proper procedure …'

The DC raises her hands, and the room goes quiet. 'It's due to our source that we got a breakthrough at all. If we don't follow through on his lead, we may lose our only chance of cracking this. What do you think, Sam?' she asks Assistant Commissioner Stirling.

Erica holds her breath, hoping her senior officer will back her.

'Erica has a point,' he says. 'We are at a critical juncture in this investigation. We need to find out who's leaking. If it's not Leon Campbell, then we're none the wiser for weeks or even months. That's time we can't afford to lose.'

DC Jones stands and addresses the three of them. 'The only people to know about this are the four of us and the commissioner. No one else. Jeff, you have 48 hours to put this in place but keep me and the assistant commissioner informed at every step. Not a word to anyone, and especially not to Murray. She's too close to Campbell.

'Jeff, Erica, you can go now.'

It's almost 10:30 pm by the time Erica gets home and pours herself a glass of wine. It's too late for dinner, but she finds a packet of brie in the back of the fridge and crackers in the pantry and decides it's as good a meal as any at this hour.

Simon is interstate at a medical conference, and she has the place to herself again, so she takes some time to replay in her head the conversations she's had with Leon since they've been working together, searching for something that hints he may not be hiding something. May be someone she can't trust. Then her thoughts turn to Laura. It's obvious she's head over heels for him, and Erica thinks Leon feels the same way about her. But what if there's some truth to what Jeff Nunn said? It would break Laura's heart, and just when she's finally opened up to someone. Since Laura brought up her concern that Simon may be up to no good, things have been strained between them, but she wouldn't wish this situation on anyone.

Exhausted, Erica tops up her glass and finishes off the cheese and biscuits. Tired as she is, she knows sleep will be a long time coming.

Shortly after 3 am, the phone rings. Groggily, Erica checks the number. It's Joel and George, the same surveillance duo that lost track of Dan. Anxiety clutches at her chest.

'What's happened?' she asks.

'There's a problem at Cain Anderson's. We've lost all vision of his property.'

'You what?'

'We haven't seen anyone coming or going, though. Should we call Tech to check what's happened?'

She hesitates, the meeting from last night playing on her mind. 'Stand by.'

Killing the call, she places another one to Assistant Commissioner Stirling.

There are five officers from the Tactical Operations Unit waiting to support her and Joel and George when Erica pulls up in front of Anderson's house. Like them, she is wearing protective gear and her firearm. The order from the Assistant Commissioner came through a few minutes earlier, authorising the arrest of Cain Anderson and search of his premises.

The tactical officers position themselves at the back and front entrances, and with everyone standing ready, Erica hammers on the door.

'Police! Open Up!'

No response. She stands back as the tactical officers ram the door open.

Straight away, the stringent smell of disinfectant hits her in the face and only gets stronger as they step through the house, guns raised, flinging open doors to the two bedrooms and bathroom.

The place has been stripped clean.

Chapter 35

Laura curls the hair framing her face and changes into a long-sleeved dark brown woollen dress that hugs her figure and accentuates her tiny waist. She completes her outfit with knee-high black leather boots. A silver necklace with a teardrop blue topaz stone and matching earrings complete her outfit as she dabs perfume on her wrists and freshens up her makeup. Critiquing her reflection in the mirror, she decides she's done the best she can with what God gave her.

She'd called Leon on the way back from Katoomba and arranged for him to come over for dinner – Thai, delivered from a local restaurant. It's almost 7:30 pm when Leon messages to say he's leaving work, and Laura spends the remaining time tidying the house before ordering the takeaway, lighting the candles and hitting a romance playlist.

Her parents' wedding song, Ben E. King's 'Stand By Me', floats through the speakers and she takes it as a good sign. Her parents met when her father was visiting family near Taree in northern New South Wales; he saw her mother's photo in the local paper and was immediately smitten. He tracked her down to the corner shop where she worked, waltzed in and asked her on a date then and there. Her mother said she couldn't help but say yes to the tall, handsome and brash man.

Six months later they were married. They both admit it was fast but fell in love the moment they met. Laura has always hoped for a love and bond as strong as theirs.

She feeds Ki and puts him to bed. By 8:30 pm, she's wondering if Leon's changed his mind when heavy footsteps approach. Swinging the door open, there he is – juggling two bags in one hand and flowers in the other.

'Delivery,' he says with a smile. 'I met the guy from the restaurant out front, so I took care of dinner. These are for you.' He hands her the bouquet of native Australian wildflowers.

'Thank you,' she says. 'You spoil me.'

As he bends down to stow a container of chocolate-dipped strawberries in the fridge, she takes the time to check him out. His beard is trimmed, and he's wearing chinos, a blue shirt that almost matches her necklace, and brown RM Williams boots. He smells like chocolate, which suggests maybe he had a hand in preparing dessert.

She pulls the wilted flowers Leon left her a few days ago from the jug she uses as a vase, tops up the water and arranges the new bouquet. Leon sets to work with the plates and glasses, and by the time he pops the champagne, Laura is so edgy she jumps at the noise.

Leon hands her a glass and kisses her, 'You look beautiful,' he murmurs as his lips travel from her mouth to her neck.

She responds to his touch and his lips, wrapping her arms around him as he lifts her and perches her on the edge of the counter. Bending down, he unzips her boots and starts massaging her feet. His fingers move up her leg toward her thigh before she places her hands on his, halting his exploration.

'I thought you wanted to?' he asks. In the candlelight, his eyes are like shining pieces of amber.

'Yes,' she breathes, 'but can we talk first?'

Leon nods, lowering his arms to rest his hands on the bench on either side of her, his face almost touching hers.

'Before we, umm, go too far,' Laura says, 'I want you to know that I've never told a partner what I've shared with you about my past and my dreams. I've always hesitated to tell anyone about it, especially someone I'm dating, in case they think I'm a nutcase. I had enough of that when I was a teenager. My dreams were stronger and more frequent then, and it got to the point I would disconnect when the visions came flooding back. It made me … different, and the other kids knew it.' Laura pauses as her breath catches in her throat. 'Even after all these years, it's hard talking about it.'

Leon rubs her arm, encouraging her to continue. 'It may sound crazy, but I feel like I've known you forever,' she says. Her mouth is suddenly dry and she swallows before continuing. 'You said you were falling for me, and I was too scared to tell you how I felt when you did, but I want to be open and honest. I'm falling for you, too.'

'You are?' Leon whispers.

'Totally,' Laura breathes.

He touches her cheek and traces the freckles on her face. 'If I put the brakes on, it's not because I don't want you. Trust me, I do. I didn't want to rush you, after what you shared about Gary, what he did and what he tried to do … to you. But I haven't felt this sure about anyone before. I haven't been able to get you out of my head since the moment we met.' He takes her hand, raises her fingers to his lips and kisses each one. 'So, are we good?'

'We're good,' she replies, with a smile of relief.

'Then there's only one last thing we need to do.' In the blink of an eye, he's swept her off the counter, carrying her in his arms. 'Find out if we both fit in that bathtub.'

Chapter 36

Laura opens her eyes and stretches. Propping her head on her hand, she watches Leon sleep. He looks younger, the lines around his eyes smoothed out in his sleep, the lids twitching as he dreams. And in that moment, she feels connected to him in a way she can't explain. The sudden rush of love catches her off guard. It's like trying to hold back the incoming tide. Impossible to stop.

Her phone vibrates: her 6 am alarm. They both have to be at work soon, but when Leon doesn't stir, she decides to leave him to sleep a little longer. She lets Ki out and feeds him before sneaking to the kitchen, where their meal from last night is sitting uneaten on the counter. She puts the containers of takeaway in the fridge before popping bread in the toaster and filling the coffee plunger. By the time she returns to bed with their breakfast, Ki is lying on the floor beside Leon, getting cuddles.

'Coffee, toast or me?' she jokes as she places the tray on the bed.

'No contest,' Leon replies, grabbing her and pulling her to him, 'but I am starving. You promised me dinner and you didn't even feed me,' he teases as he shoves half a piece of marmalade toast into his mouth.

'I didn't hear any complaints last night,' Laura retorts as they both reach for the same slice.

By 7:50 am, the three of them are riding the lift up to the office. The daily team briefing isn't for another 10 minutes, but as the doors slide open, they're greeted by Matt, who appears to have been waiting for them.

'Morning,' he says, and indicates they should follow him to the briefing room. 'You're just in time – we're starting early.'

Erica is sitting at the head of the table, and Laura can tell straight away that something is wrong. Loose strands of hair have escaped her normally neat bun and she's tapping her fingers on the table. But what worries her more is the way Erica doesn't acknowledge either her or Leon when they enter the room. A telltale rush of colour creeps up Laura's neck as she catches Alex's eye and receives a wry smile in return.

'Right. Now that everyone is here,' Erica begins. Her tone reminds Laura of being scolded by her parents; it's not like they were late. 'We've had some major developments overnight. Cain Anderson has vanished. Somehow, he interrupted our surveillance feeds and got out of his house unnoticed, stripping the place clean and bleaching what was left to get rid of anything forensics might use.'

'Boss,' Leon cuts in, 'you should have called me. I would have come in and checked what was going on.'

'We didn't have time.'

Leon opens his mouth to respond but Laura pokes him under the table and he thinks better of it.

'This is the situation. Our informant is missing, and now our main lead and suspect has disappeared too. So, this is what we need to do. Joel and George, I want you to return to watching Anderson's house, just in case he decides to return. Leon, I'd like you and your team to review the footage from the house last night. Check for anyone the surveillance team may have missed before they lost access. And I want an explanation by midday for why we lost vision in the first place.'

Worry and disappointment darken Leon's face and Laura instinctively knows what he's thinking – that he may have stuffed up and let everyone down. She wants to hold him and tell him everything will be okay, but she can't. They need to remain professional.

The room empties as the various teams scurry off until only Laura and Erica remain. 'What would you like me to do?' she asks in a quiet voice.

For the first time that morning, Erica looks directly at her. 'Alex said she's asked you to start working closely with the officer in charge at Armidale station. I'd like you to see what you can find out. I need any leads we can get.'

Laura nods and makes to leave but pauses at the doorway. 'Are you okay, Erica? I know you must be disappointed, but it feels like something else is going on. We're good, aren't we?'

Gathering her papers and laptop, Erica lowers her eyes as she replies. 'It's been a long night, and it's going to be a long day. That's all.'

'I've heard a lot about you,' Senior Sergeant Fuller tells Laura. 'Superintendent Hewson's an old friend. He speaks highly of you.'

Laura smiles into the phone. 'That's good to know, thank you. And Superintendent Hewson was most helpful too. We got some valuable leads while we were in Leeton.'

'So how can I help you?'

'I've pulled some initial information from public and police reports about criminal activity in the area to help build a picture of what's been going on but we'd like to follow the same investigative path with Tori Engel as we did with Sophie Romano,' Laura explains. 'Starting with access to the records of interviews with Tori's family, friends and colleagues.'

'Not a problem.'

'We'd also like some information about where she works. There were some interesting facts we unearthed about the winery where Sophie Romano performs, and we're considering links to workplaces of the other missing women.'

Fuller considers a while. 'It's an old heritage pub called The Drovers Arms. It closed a couple of years ago before it was brought back to life by Andy Briginshaw, a well-known Sydney property tycoon. He spared no expense, that's for sure. He revamped the bistro, beer garden and the bars, and brought in a fancy chef and new kitchen crew. Put in a stage and all the gear for live bands to play. Now it's popular with pretty much everyone, locals and visitors. What's your email?'

Laura spells the address out down the line and a moment or two later there's a ping from her inbox. She opens the message and finds there's an attachment: an article from the lifestyle pages of *The Armidale Express* featuring the re-opening of the pub in January this year after almost 18 months of renovation. Laura sets the story itself aside for later but first takes a close look at the accompanying photo: billionaire Andy Briginshaw holding a jug of beer in front of a crowded main bar. The mayor stands to one side of him, and behind the bar is Tori Engel.

'Thank you,' Laura says. 'Is there anything you can tell us about the dance studio where Tori was a teacher?'

'It's owned by Irina Stepanova, a former Russian prima ballerina, believe it or not,' Fuller says. 'She married a rich Australian farmer and ran the dance studio for more than 40 years. She's over 80, long since retired, and her daughter is in charge now. I'll dig up some more information and send it through.'

'I'd really appreciate that,' Laura replies, warming to Fuller's kindness and willingness to go out of her way for her requests.

'Anytime. Let me know if you need anything else. And if you and Ki want to pop by and check anything else out in person, let me know. We'll be happy to have you.'

It takes about 15 minutes for Laura to fill Alex in on what she's learned, the detective listening in attentive silence as she runs through her conversation with Senior Sergeant Fuller.

'Reckon we need to have our analyst look into this billionaire pub owner,' Alex says when Laura has finished. 'Maybe he's been getting some financial help from unusual sources too. And the dance school could do with a look as well.' She picks up her phone and dials Adam, the financial expert digging into the Leeton winery bailout. He answers on the second ring and Alex puts the call on speaker.

'Alex,' he says, not waiting for her to explain why she's calling. 'I was just about to ring you. Got some more details about the company that funded the Larsons' vineyard.'

'Great,' Alex says. 'What do you know?'

'It appears that in addition to the Larsons, the Manila company that sorted their debt out has also invested in several niche software companies that specialise in data encryption and protection,' he says. 'But that's just the tip of the iceberg. The company portfolio includes a whole lot of vineyards, hotels and nightclubs.'

'And here we were just about to ask you to look into that,' Alex says.

'No problem. If you've got names of businesses, email them to me and I'll cross-check. But that's not the most interesting news.'

Alex sits forward in her seat. 'Oh?'

'The woman fronting the company is Susie Morton. She uses her maiden name or we'd have twigged sooner that she's married to Gian Russo, better known as John Russo.'

Alex's face creases in thought. 'Why does that name ring a bell?'

'Because he's currently the subject of a joint investigation for suspected major money laundering activities by several law enforcement agencies, including the NSW Police, the Australian Federal Police, the Australian Criminal Intelligence Commission, the Australian Tax Office and AUSTRAC, probably.'

'Yes, that'll be it,' Alex quips.

AUSTRAC, Laura recalls, is the national financial intelligence agency. Whoever this guy is, he's a big target.

'While he was born in Australia, he has family ties to Calabria,' Adam goes on. 'It's believed many of the businesses his Manila company have funded may be a front for money laundering, including the Larsons' winery. I'll be talking to the other agencies and seeking access to any records or material they can share, especially anything that points to interactions with Sophie Romano or her family.'

As she listens, Alex's fingers rattle over the keyboard of her computer. In an instant, she's brought up a profile of the property tycoon from two years ago on a well-known online real estate website. 'That'll be great,' she says, turning the screen so Laura can read it. 'And I'll send you the details of those businesses I need looking into.'

'Can't wait,' Adam says, without a trace of sarcasm.

Alex hangs up as Laura scans the internet article. The Sydney property magnate spends most of it chatting about the challenges of the luxury property market and refers to one of his biggest moments – the record-breaking sale of a Sydney harbourside home during a period of sustained interest rate rises, and when luxury homes sat on the market with little interest from buyers. There's a photo of him standing in front of an infinity pool with the Harbour Bridge in the background. Beside him are the new owners, Susie Morton and John Russo, the husband and wife who invested in the Larsons' winery.

'I'll update Erica on this latest development,' Alex says. 'Can you follow up with Armidale station and confirm timing for a visit? We need to explore every avenue.'

'Of course,' Laura says. 'I'll get on it.'

When Laura returns to her desk, Leon's not there.

'He's just ducked out for a meeting,' Jess says without glancing up from her workstation.

'Who with?'

'Didn't say.'

Laura shrugs and sits at her own desk, checks her messages and emails. As she starts to read, her desk phone lights up with an incoming call. She checks the screen but doesn't recognise the number. After a short internal debate between ignoring it and letting them leave a message or taking the call, Laura picks up.

'Senior Constable Murray? Jacob Henley. We met in Katoomba …'

'I remember,' Laura says, continuing to scroll through her emails. 'To what do I owe this pleasure?'

'I had a call from Cate Bell this morning,' Jacob says. 'It's pretty odd to get a call from a member of the public in my job, even one I've rescued, but she insisted she had to share something with me.'

Something in the tone of his voice makes Laura stop filtering her inbox and pay attention. 'She said she's just remembered something from before she fell and thinks it might be important to the police. I thought I'd better listen to what she had to say. Took the precaution of recording it too.'

'Okay,' Laura says. 'And you think it's something I can help with?' She wonders where this is going. No one outside the party who found Dan's head and the forensic team that recovered it knows about what Ki discovered during the search.

'Well, I remembered you saying you're seconded to Taskforce Lacuna in headquarters, and I figured if anyone would know who to pass this on to, you would. I'm out of the loop in Dubbo, I don't know who's who,' he laughs.

'All right,' she replies, dragging a notepad and pen towards her. 'Why don't you tell me what Ms Bell said. I'm not sure if it will be relevant for the taskforce, but I'll figure out where it needs to go.'

'Right,' Jacob begins. 'Cate said she suffered some memory loss from her concussion after the accident, but things have been coming back to her in bits and pieces. She admitted going off the main track was a dumb move, but it seems some others had the same stupid idea. She remembered people were trekking through the bush about 200 metres away but she hid from them because they looked like the sort of guys you don't mess with, and after all the media coverage about women going missing, she was cautious. There were three of them – one of them was carrying a bag and the other two were following him. She said the man at the back was laughing, saying something about leaving gifts.'

Laura tenses. 'Did she describe them?'

'She managed to sneak a picture on her phone,' Jacob replies, 'but it was smashed to bits when she fell. Luckily, she set up a function so any photos she takes are automatically uploaded to the Cloud, that way she can sync them on her laptop and other devices.'

'So, you've got the picture?' Laura surges with excitement.

'Sure do. Want me to send it to you?'

'Absolutely! And the record of your conversation with Cate, please.'

She confirms her email address and thanks Jacob for the call, promising she'll get the information in front of the right people, then ends the call and waits. Soon, the image lands in her inbox, but her spirits drop instantly when she opens it. The picture is so fuzzy you'd never guess Cate was a keen photographer. The only explanation is that she must have waited until the men had walked well ahead before taking it, and in her nervous state, forgotten to zoom in.

The image is of the backs of three men; a dark blob around the neck of one of them she suspects is a tattoo. Can it be enhanced?

Saving the photo she sends it to Erica. Maybe this is the break she needs after the disasters of the last few hours.

Chapter 37

Erica's mood improves after Laura tells her about the picture. Her instinct to bring Laura and Ki onto the taskforce had been questioned by others who wondered what value the pair would bring to the team, but Laura's natural ability to forge relationships has delivered some great leads. Her innate sense to follow her gut is also paying off, and Erica holds out hope their upcoming visit to Armidale may be another turning point.

Then there's the promising financial investigation from Alex, confirming someone with potential links to the Australian mafia may be connected to at least two of the locations and businesses where women have gone missing. Erica is quietly confident they'll find more. And while they haven't nailed who the other big players are, there is a link between the Scorpions and the operation's main salesman, Cain Anderson.

She wonders about the image Laura sent her. The blur Laura thinks is a tattoo might be the thing that places the Scorpions at the location where Dan's head was found – if she can identify the man in the picture as Merlin.

But how to do that? Usually, she would send the picture straight to Leon, but the conversation with Professional Standards spooked her more than she'd like to admit. She could be showing her hand to the enemy.

Yet if she deviates from her normal process, Leon and his team will wonder why. He's already questioned why she didn't call him to check why they lost the feed from Anderson's last night.

Attaching the image to an email, she sends it to the head of her technical team with instructions to clean it up, top priority.

By the end-of-day briefing with the DC and Assistant Commissioner, Erica is struggling to maintain her focus. Internally, she blames lack of sleep and high stress. Having been congratulated on her progress so far, and encouraged to push even harder, she stands to leave but is immediately overcome by dizziness. Dots swim before her eyes, and she has to grab the table to stop from swaying.

DC Jones rushes to her side, easing her down onto the couch. 'Erica, when did you last sleep?' she asks. 'Or eat?'

Leaning over with her head between her legs, Erica says nothing, waiting for the light-headedness to pass.

Jones turns to address Stirling. 'I'm recommending that Erica take a day off. Effective now. I'll need you to step in and take the lead, Sam.'

'No, no, I'm all right,' Erica protests. 'It was just a dizzy spell. I'll get some sleep tonight, have some dinner. I'll be right in the morning.'

'I'm sure you will,' Jones counters, 'but I don't want to see your face in here until Monday. That gives you tomorrow and the whole weekend to recover. And if you don't stay out of the office and offline, I'll make you take more time off. Do you understand?'

'But we're at a critical point …' Erica begins.

'And Assistant Commissioner Stirling is very experienced and capable. I'm sure he and Detective Jeffries will keep things ticking over in your absence.'

Erica bites her tongue and nods. Arguing with the DC is not a good career move, even if she's convinced the senior officer is fretting needlessly.

'Good. I'm glad you're being sensible. Then I want you back here on Monday, fully operational and raring to go. And no weekend work! I'll be watching. Now I'm ordering you – go home and rest.'

Chapter 38

The aroma of freshly brewed coffee wafts to the lounge room, rousing Erica from her slumber. As soon as she got home, she'd changed into her pyjamas and stretched out on the couch, wrapping herself in a blanket. She'd started watching a movie but soon fell asleep.

Rubbing her eyes, she recognises Simon's voice, low and muted, chatting on the phone. She rises from the lounge, yawning, and pads barefoot across the polished wood floor to the kitchen. It's still dark outside.

'Right then. I'll be in soon,' Simon says into the phone before placing it back in his pocket. He smiles at Erica, a contrite look on his face, and hands her a camomile tea as she perches on the stool at the island bench next to him. 'I'm sorry, sweetheart. I didn't mean to wake you.'

'I didn't hear you come home. What time is it? I must have really crashed. Have you been called in again?' she asks, trying to hide her disappointment.

'It's after 10 pm. I've been home for a couple of hours, but I didn't want to wake you. One of my patients has gone downhill, a young child. It's serious.' He rests his hand on her knee and rubs the soft wool covering her skin.

'Maybe you can get away once you've sorted it out,' she suggests. 'I was hoping we could go to dinner this evening but it's too late now. But maybe you could chuck a sickie tomorrow and we could spend the day together? I never take a day off and it's been ages since we spent quality time together.' She places her hand over his and moves it up her leg.

'Leading Senior Constable, I can't believe you're encouraging me to dodge work,' Simon laughs as Erica leans in and places her other hand on his bum, pushing him closer. 'Don't tempt me!' Simon groans as he stands up. 'I promise I'll get away as soon as I can. In the meantime, the least I can do is cook you something before I go. What do you feel like?'

'Anything at all,' Erica says, her stomach grumbling, a reminder that it's been a while since she's had any proper sustenance.

'We really need to do a shop,' he mumbles as he searches the pantry and fridge for something to cook. Finally, he pulls out a carton of eggs. 'It's going to have to be an omelette, I hope that's okay.'

'Sure is. I'd eat anything at this point,' Erica replies as she watches him flick through playlists on his phone. He chooses an 80s retro mix, then sets to whisking eggs and spices in a bowl before pouring the mixture into a pan and crumbling some leftover feta and olives into it. Waving the spatula in the air, he wiggles his bottom in time to George Michael's *Faith* while Erica enjoys the show.

He really does have a cute bottom.

She's so hungry she wolfs the feast down as soon as it's ready. But as Simon pours her a glass of wine, her stomach somersaults, the meal rising in her throat. She rushes to the bathroom, making it just in time before vomiting. Clutching the toilet bowl, she waits for the heaving to stop before wiping her mouth and flushing.

'Are you all right?' Simon asks from the doorway.

'Don't come in. It's not pretty and smells worse.' She pulls herself to the basin and grabs her toothbrush.

'Hey, I'm a doctor, remember. I deal with "not pretty and smelly" every day.' He steps into the bathroom and rubs her back. 'Those eggs weren't out of date, were they?'

'I don't think so,' Erica says. 'I think I just ate them too fast.' She splashes water over her face as Simon returns to the kitchen to check the eggs.

'No, all good,' he says, waving the carton in the air. 'Might be a tummy bug. Want me to stay home and look after you?'

'I'll be fine,' he replies. 'And that patient of yours needs you more.'

Simon raids his medicine bag and hands her two tablets and a large glass of water. 'These will settle your stomach. Now go to bed and stay hydrated. Doctor's orders.'

'Yes, sir,' Erica says, and gets into bed as he closes the blinds and places a bottle of water on the bedside table.

'I'll message you later, to check how you're doing,' he says as he changes into fresh scrubs. He kisses her gently on the forehead, and a wave of tiredness washes over her. The dizzy spell yesterday and now this. She's been pushing herself so hard, it's no wonder her body is telling her to slow down.

Snuggling under the doona, her eyes are already closing; she doesn't even hear Simon leave.

Chapter 39

The ping of her phone wakes Laura shortly before 6 am. Holding the handset in front of her bleary eyes, she sees the text is from Erica.

MEET ME OUT FRONT IN 15?
ON LEAVE TODAY BUT WOULD LIKE TO BUY YOU BREAKFAST. WANT TO TALK ABOUT SIMON.

Laura reaches across to the other side of the bed, her fingers rubbing against the cold sheet. Leon messaged her the night before, saying he was having to work late and not to wait up, but she still feels his absence deep inside herself. On the other hand, she has no plans for breakfast now, so she texts back.

SURE.

Her phone beeps again a moment later.

YOU'LL HAVE TO LEAVE KI. CAFÉ ISN'T DOG FRIENDLY. SORRY.

Odd, Laura thinks, wracking her brains about which coffee shops around here didn't at least let dogs sit outside, but she only has 15 minutes to get ready and dressed, so she quickly feeds Ki and lets him out for his morning business before bringing him back inside.

'I'll be back soon,' she reassures him, lavishing him with pats. Then she grabs her bag and heads out.

She's been standing on the pavement for five minutes, scanning the street for Erica's car, when a white SUV pulls up to the kerb. Before she can react, the back doors are flung open, and she's bundled inside, a bag rammed down over her head.

Lashing out, she hears a low moan as her elbow connects with one of her captors, and she opens her mouth to scream – hoping someone outside is watching, witnessing what's happening. Before any sound escapes, something heavy smashes into her head and she slides unconscious onto the seat.

There's a weird mustiness in the air, the sort of smell that seeps into every corner of a house that's been boarded up for too long. Soft notes of classical music reach Laura's ears, and she cracks open her eyes.

It's dark, but she can tell she's lying on satin sheets, the feel of them distinct against her bare skin. Gradually, her brain registers that she's bound hand and foot to the bedposts, tape over her mouth, and panic reaches out to grab her. She almost lets it, but then her training kicks in and she starts counting her heartbeats to slow her racing pulse. If she wants to get out of here, she has to remain calm. Find out where she is. Who's she with. What's happened.

Light streams in as a door opens and for a brief moment she catches the outline of a man's face, the lower half covered by a face mask, before the door closes again.

The mattress sags as the man kneels on the bed, and she senses rather than sees him lean over her. Rough fingers tuck her hair behind her ears, and she gags under the tape from the cheap aftershave that fails to mask the man's pungent body odour.

'Let's get a better look at you,' he says, and a soft glow illuminates her skin as he sweeps a phone over her body. 'You are cute. Even better looking out of uniform,' he teases.

She thrashes against the ropes, but his bony fingers dig into her cheeks painfully and he turns her face to his. 'Now, now, sweetheart. Behave. Show everyone how lovely you are.'

His voice is familiar, but her brain won't function properly, like a car engine struggling to turn over on a cold winter's morning. Then, in the warm light of the camera-phone, she recognises his eyes, and the engine fires.

She wriggles away, and he chuckles. 'Figured out who I am, have you? Oh, you'll wish you'd never tried to mess with me, girl.'

Laura continues to strain against the ropes, but Cain Anderson merely laughs. 'You really are a fighter, aren't you? I have something that can help with that.'

She winces at the pain in her arm before sliding back into the darkness.

Something cold touches her chest, like icicles over her heart.

A man is stooped over her, stethoscope in his ears.

Simon.

The ice tightens behind her ribs.

'Don't struggle,' he whispers. 'It will only make things worse.'

She tries to shout out, but the duct tape steals her words away, and she's reduced to shaking her head from side to side, yelling obscenities he'll never hear.

The door opens, and she swivels her head to look at the newcomer – Cain Anderson, but this time he's not alone. A tall woman with ash-blonde shoulder-length hair, blue eyes and a diamond nose piercing follows close behind him.

'How's she doin', Doc?' Cain asks.

'Heart rate is steadying,' Simon replies, backing away from the bed. 'She has a concussion, not helped by the sedative, but she's recovering well. There shouldn't be any permanent damage.'

Cain pulls a chair to the bedside and sits. Laura freezes as he runs his fingers over the soft material of her bra and down her stomach toward her navel. The blonde woman hovers in the doorway, smirking at her discomfiture.

'You know the saying, be careful what you wish for,' Cain mocks. 'Well, you lot wanted to know who was pulling the strings, who was running this gig. Let me introduce you.' He motions to the woman, who approaches the foot of the bed and leans on the ornate, antique bedframe. She stares at her captive, a curious expression on her face.

'You don't know who I am, do you, *Laura*?' she sneers. 'And here I thought you were smart. You'd have to be, to be involved in a high-profile police operation at such a young age, right?'

Laura remains still, holding the woman's gaze while sifting her confused mind for a connection. Clearly, she was supposed to recognise her, but she can't place the face. She sweeps her eyes over the woman, seeking another clue; tight black crop top that shows off perfectly round bosoms, slim waist, pouty full lips that hint at regular botox and baggy, ripped designer jeans.

Nothing that helps.

'Maybe you're not that bright after all,' the woman goes on. 'Maybe you're just privileged. Life served up on a silver platter. A happy family home, showered with love, good education, the right friends.' She leans in, eyes piercing Laura's soul. 'Very different to me. But we'll get to that. Tell me, how does it feel to be betrayed by someone you thought was a friend?'

She nods at Simon, who sidles to her side. Grabbing him by the waist, she pulls him against her hips and kisses him, the exchange long and deep.

'He's one hell of a lover,' she says when she breaks for air. 'You should tell your boss. Oh, but she already knows, doesn't she? She was never suspicious of Simon … but you were, weren't you? He told me you were snooping around.'

The blush of anger colours Laura's cheeks and she pictures herself handcuffing and arresting them all. It works; the thought of revenge calms her. If she has any chance of getting out of this alive, she needs to stay composed. Stay alert.

'Nothing to say? Oh, that's right, you can't,' the woman cackles. 'Cain, remove the tape. I'd like to hear what the Senior Constable has to say. If she tries to scream, it'll be the last sound she makes.'

Cain rips the tape off, and Laura's lips bleed as pieces of skin peel away with it. She rubs her tongue across her mouth before Cain lifts her head and pours water down her throat. Coughing and spluttering from the sudden intake of fluids, she slumps onto the bed, wincing as the lump at the back of her head hits the mattress.

'Who are you?' Laura croaks.

'Ah. Now that is an interesting question, isn't it? Are you honestly interested in my story?'

Laura nods. The woman motions for Cain to get up and takes his seat by the bed. 'All right then. I mean, you're not going to tell anyone, so why not?

'Growing up, I got mixed up with a rough crowd in Melbourne. My mum was a junkie and my older brother was the leader of a gang, but he took off when he turned 18. That left me in a world of fending off predators, of playing the victim, and it didn't take long before I got sick of that. So, I took back control. I set up my own business. Escorts. It was a small operation at first, just a handful of girls, but I hand-picked the women, offering the best possible product. High-class hookers that would fulfil any fantasy for a fee.

'It's amazing what men are willing to pay for a top-shelf service where the women will do whatever they want. Demand grew, and I expanded interstate. Word got out, then I had a visit from the 'Ndrangheta. They weren't happy I was taking business from their brothels. So, we agreed – I'd give them a cut of the profits in return for their protection and keeping the cops off our backs.

'That's how I met my old partner, Joe. He was in the inner circle and came to sample the merchandise. He was impressed, but I impressed him more.' She smirks at the memory.

'He didn't last long, though. Got himself knocked off. Long story, I won't bore you with it. Anyway, there I was, vulnerable and having to prove my worth. Again. So, I pitched an idea to their boss. It was something I'd thought about and even tried before but didn't have the means or support to be successful. I knew with the right connections and people I could make it work this time.

'I outlined my plan and they went for it. I'd supply pretty young Australian women for … well, I like to call it re-homing. The girls get a new identity and fetch a high price on our marketplace on the dark web. They agreed to trial it, and for the last six months, I've used the society's contacts and links with other criminal groups to source the right kind of merchandise.'

She motions to Simon to sit on the bed with her. He complies, and she pulls him close, placing her hand on his crotch. 'One of the problems I had to iron out was how to keep the women calm and compliant.' A distant look settles over her face. 'Ally Webster.'

Laura's mind races. Ally, the first girl to go missing, years before the others.

'You'd be surprised how easy it is to overdose someone. I needed a professional to help me out.' Her rubbing between Simon's legs increases. 'Loverboy here filled my gap perfectly.'

Laura's eyes flick to his face. He has the decency to look ashamed at least.

'Your boss probably told you all about Simon's poor life as a boy. How he never knew his father. Rubbish, of course. He tracked down daddy dearest, but not before his father had drunk himself to death. We helped him find his dad, you know?

'How could we refuse when Simon was so desperate? His father was a good-looking rooster, a trait Simon shares. They also share something else. Debts. Daddy was not only a big drinker – he was a compulsive gambler. The society paid off his outstanding debts to bookies but he didn't live long enough to hold up his side of the bargain. So, when Simon came along, we made it clear he had an obligation to clean his old man's slate. As an added extra, we also paid off his uni fees. He's been repaying his debts by supplying drugs to sedate the women and keeping them healthy until delivery. Docile and hidden while I generated interest and demand in the marketplace. You know, he's even helping me find new stock now? That cute little nurse he met at a hospital fundraiser, Meg Harrison. She was one of his. He told me about another a few days ago. So eager to please me. But it would look too suspicious if another nurse went missing, especially one who works at the same hospital.

'But imagine when he told me about you. How your boss had put you on her payroll. I couldn't believe my luck.'

The blonde woman rubs her forefinger along Laura's mouth before sucking on it. 'You see, you knew my big brother. Gary Wilson.'

Laura gasps, and in that moment, she sees the resemblance. The blonde has the same shaped face, even down to the dimple in her chin, the same colour and tilt of eyes.

'You remember him. How sweet. He talked about you, you know, when he was in prison. Filled me in on how you told the police about his attempt to get to you. Your testimony and the trap that Martin bitch laid for him. And now the two of you work together!'

'All my brother talked about was vengeance, and now I get to deliver it.'

'Funny,' Laura says. 'He never mentioned you.'

The woman's face darkens, and Simon puts a hand on her upper arm to calm her. 'Karlie,' he breathes.

Karlie's features settle again; his intervention has done the trick. 'Simon's right. I want you to experience what the women you so desperately wanted to save have been through. You're not a stunner, but you do have a wholesome, girl-next-door vibe. If you were a virgin, demand would be through the roof, but Simon tells me that ship has sailed. Doesn't matter; you're already generating a lot of interest from buyers. An innocent-looking, cute copper they can play with all day and all night.

'I mean, I do still want to kill you.' She bends down and picks up a large rock from the floor, weighing it in her hands. She holds the rock to the light, examining the different colours and pieces embedded in its surface before returning her gaze to Laura. 'Do it like my brother used to, by pounding you to death with a rock from the gorge where he lived. I even brought this one from there specially. But no.' She sighs. 'Life is full of difficult choices, isn't it?'

The malice, the hatred surges from this woman like poison and Laura is in no doubt Karlie will relish every moment of torturing her. So, if her choice is between becoming a sex slave or dying, Laura chooses the latter.

'You're so keen to avenge him? You meant nothing to him.' she says, her voice low and even. 'He *left* you. The only person he cared for was himself. That's the thing about psychopaths, they're incapable of love. You were nothing to him.'

Placing the rock on the bed, Karlie leans so close that Laura can count her false eyelashes. Lifting a lock of Laura's hair, she sniffs it. 'Nice try, but you didn't know my brother. You were merely another trophy for his collection.'

Laura turns her head toward Simon. 'You're better than this. You're a doctor. You help others, you don't hurt them. I told Erica I thought you were up to something, but she didn't believe me because she loves you. She believes in you. Don't do this. Don't let *her*,' she tilts her chin to indicate Karlie, 'turn you into a villain.'

Simon's eyes drop to the ground. Then he gets up and walks out.

'Do you seriously think you can get away with this?' Laura calls after him.

'Sweet thing, we already have,' Karlie laughs. 'Now, all this chit-chat is making me horny, and Simon clearly needs something to cheer him up.' She stands and turns to Cain.

'Tape her up again.'

Chapter 40

It's after 11 pm by the time Leon has used all his technical prowess to enhance the shoddy photo Erica sent him.

While it's still pixelated, through meticulous digital refinement, he got it to the point where he could run it through facial recognition and image-matching software.

It came back as indicating there is a high probability that the man with the tattoo is Merlin, the Scorpions' moneyman and friend of Cain Anderson. Rubbing his tired eyes, Leon sends the enhanced image and analysis back to his boss.

Erica hadn't told him why he needed to work on the photo so urgently, only that he should make it a priority. Matt had offered to help, but while the work was intense, it was a one-man job, and Leon had sent his team home. Besides, after the debacle of losing all vision at Anderson's property, he was determined to stay up all night to get a result. Now, sitting in the darkened office, he realises it's been hours since he spoke to Laura, but he resists the urge to message his girlfriend.

Girlfriend.

It's the first time, even in his mind, that he's labelled their relationship. But he likes it.

He messages her as soon as he wakes the next morning, telling her how much he missed her last night and how he's keen for a coffee run after the morning briefing. But by the time he's parking in the basement of the office building, there's still been no response. Climbing out of the car, he checks his phone again, then heads up in the lift.

The only person at their desk is Jess.

'Have you heard from Laura or Matt?' he asks.

'I just took a call from Matt. He sounded tired and said he was throwing up all night, so he won't be in. No sign of Laura and Ki. You coming to the briefing?'

'Right. Yes. I'll be there in a minute,' Leon mutters. He drops his bag, logs on and checks his emails, wondering if Laura and Ki have been called out on another urgent job and she didn't have time to let him know. But there's nothing in his inbox either that sheds any light, so he locks his screen, grabs his notebook and races to the daily briefing.

Assistant Commissioner Stirling is sitting in Erica's spot, Alex by his side. Jess gives him a quizzical look, and he shrugs in response.

Looking around the table, Stirling frowns. 'Is this it? Is everyone here?'

'Matt is unwell,' Leon explains. 'He won't be in.'

'And where's Senior Constable Murray?' the senior officer asks, directing the question to Leon.

'I'm not sure, sir. I haven't seen her since yesterday afternoon.'

'Detective, have you heard from Murray? The senior officer asks Alex.

'Not today, no.'

'I thought maybe she was sent to an urgent job. Perhaps another search operation?' Leon suggests.

'There's been no request for assistance,' Stirling muses. 'Alex, please call Murray as soon as we're finished and find out why she hasn't turned up.'

Alex nods, and, satisfied, the assistant commissioner begins the meeting. 'Your team leader is on leave today. She'll be returning Monday, so I'm in charge in her absence—for today and over the weekend. So, updates.'

At the end of the briefing, Leon waits for everyone to leave and asks Stirling if he can talk to him privately.

'Did Erica tell you about the photo she wanted me to work on last night?'

'She did,' Stirling answers, one eyebrow raised. 'I wondered why you left that out of your report.'

'She didn't tell me much about the image, or what she wanted it for,' Leon explains. 'I wasn't sure how many people were aware of it or should know about it, so I didn't want to raise it.'

'Understood,' his senior officer says, and there's something in his expression that makes Leon wonder if there's even more to this than he's guessing.

'I sent Erica an email late last night, informing her there's a high probability one of the men in the shot is the Scorpion's bikie known as Merlin.'

'Good work. Send it through to me as soon as you get back to your desk and keep it to yourself for now.' He moves to the door but Leon positions himself between the senior officer and the exit.

'Sir, I'm not sure if you know but Laura, I mean Senior Constable Murray, and I are … well, we're in a relationship.'

'I had heard something to that effect. Congratulations.'

'Well, the thing is, sir, I didn't see her yesterday evening, and she didn't respond to my message early this morning.'

'Your point being?'

'It's not like her. I mean, we're … we're in the early days of our relationship. We're always in touch. You know.' Leon tries to find some common experience of the honeymoon period of dating, but Stirling's expression stays blank. 'It's not like her. And if she's not on a job …'

'She could be sick. Hardly time to call to send out a search party,' Stirling says. 'Now, was there anything else?'

'Yes, sir,' Leon replies, closing the door behind him. His hands shake as he flicks open his notebook. 'I suspect someone has been accessing information on my computer.'

That gets Stirling's attention. 'Go on.'

'Before I lock down my machine, I jot into my notebook what time I log on and off each day. I note when I restart the following day. To keep track of my hours and my online activity. The thing is, someone logged in while I was away from my desk and didn't sign off properly. And the only person in our area at that time was Matt. And there was another occasion when I thought I must have slipped up, not logged off properly, but when I looked at the activity on my machine, the timeframes didn't add up.'

'Matt is your man who called in sick today?'

'Yes, sir.' Leon takes a deep breath before continuing, 'I don't know how he got access. I secure all my passwords and change them regularly. But Matt had applied to the cyber unit before he got a job with my team, and he's doing an IT degree part-time. Maybe he's a better hacker than I thought.'

The older man's eyes narrow like he's debating whether to believe Leon or not. 'Do you have any hard evidence to back that up?'

'He's been acting a bit off lately, disappearing at odd times. I think I have enough to justify checking him out. I hate to think anyone in my team would do something like that but first our source disappears and then Anderson vanishes.' *And now Laura's not responding.* 'You don't have to be Einstein to work out we have a mole.'

'Hmm. I see,' Stirling murmurs. He's about to go on when Alex knocks on the door before pushing it open.

'I can't get hold of Murray,' she says. 'She's not answering her phone or messages on our team app.' There's an unmistakable note of concern in her voice. 'She's usually very responsive and responsible.'

Stirling looks from her to Leon and back. 'Take a seat, Detective,' he says. 'We need to have a serious discussion.'

Chapter 41

Perched on the edge of his chair, nose close to the screen, headphones on, Leon watches the live feed as Alex pulls up to the kerb behind Laura's car.

Alex gets out of her vehicle, strides to Laura's car and tries the door. Locked. She peers through the window as she waits for two of the surveillance crew, Kate and Hannah, to join her, then all three officers approach the small two-bedroom cottage.

They open the gate to the path, reaching for their weapons. Leon's told them there's only one way in and out: the front door and that Laura has been renting the place situated at the back of her uncle's property since moving to Sydney.

Alex raps on the wood. 'Laura, are you home? Are you there?'

Ki barks in response, and Leon swallows, his throat dry. 'She wouldn't leave him alone for long,' he says into his headset.

Alex stands back as Kate, the older of the two officers, finesses the lock and eases the door open. Ki pushes his nose through the gap. Alex soothes the excited canine, who jumps up and down before pushing past her to relieve himself, then racing back inside.

After a swift search of the premises, it's obvious Laura's not there and there's no sign of any struggle or break-in.

'Alex,' Leon says, a heavy weight settling in his gut, 'the couple who live across the road have security cameras. Laura told me they asked her advice a few months back on what to install.'

'Acknowledged,' Alex says, and the feed on her body cam shows her crossing the street and knocking at the door. Leon catches a glimpse of the cameras and prays they're working and that they capture footage from the street.

'Good morning,' Alex says, flashing her badge at the older woman who opens the door. 'My name is Detective Alex Jeffries, and I'm wondering if you could help me.'

Pattie Nichols summons her husband, Graham, and they set to work retrieving the footage from their cameras. Pattie plugs a charger into a small tablet, and the couple argue about the password to the device; Leon starts deep breathing, to stop himself from yelling at Alex to hurry them up. At last, Pattie digs a small diary out of her handbag and flicks to the back page; she calls out the password for Graham's bumbling fingers to type in.

Taking control of the security app, Alex speeds through the footage from sun-up onwards. At around 6:20 am, the camera captures Laura, in uniform, leaving the house. Leon follows

236

Laura as she walks to the road, watches as she peers up and down the street, looking for someone. She checks her phone, then a white SUV pulls up to the kerb. As the back doors swing open, two men in black and wearing balaclavas jump out and thrust her into the vehicle, before it swings around and speeds off the way it came.

'Rewind three seconds,' Leon instructs Alex. She does as requested and Leon takes a screenshot of the number plate as the car turns around. 'Now go back to when the two people get out of the car.' His voice wavers as he tries to dampen the panic that's rising inside him.

They watch the two men leap out of the vehicle. Their faces are obscured and they're wearing black leather gloves, long pants and jackets. The first one is shorter, slightly hunched and his movements are slower. The second is tall and moves with quick precision. He's wearing what looks like black cargo pants with pockets down each side.

'Detective,' Leon says. 'I think one of those men is wearing scrubs.'

Chapter 42

Dark. It's so dark. The block-out blinds they installed so Simon can get a decent sleep after night shifts mean Erica has no chance of working out what time of the day it is or how long she's slept for.

Her head pounds like she has a horrible migraine, and she reaches for her water, guzzles what's left in the bottle.

The other side of the bed is cold and empty.

'Simon, are you home?' No response. He must still be at the hospital.

As she sits up, another dizzy spell hits, and she leans over, grasping her knees. Maybe she has a virus. She can count on one hand the number of sick days she's had in her life, but feeling like this, she's willing to admit she'll need a few days off.

Her fingers reach out to the bedside table where her phone is charging. Except it isn't. *Damn.* She must have forgotten to plug it in. It'll be in her handbag.

On wobbly legs, she heads down the hallway to the bathroom; there's daylight coming from the small window in the kitchen, but without her phone, there's still no way for her to tell the time. Her stomach grumbles but the thought of food still makes her feel ill. Instead, she takes a long, hot shower and, wrapped in a towel, returns to their room.

Flicking on the bedroom light, she realises the contents of her bag are strewn across the floor. It was so dark and she was so out of it, she hadn't noticed before.

Her phone is missing.

Pulse racing, she searches the room for her laptop. Gone. The wardrobe door is ajar, and she flings it open to find empty hangers and clean shelves on Simon's side.

She runs to his study, pushes open the door. The cabinet drawers are open and empty, and a dusty outline on the desk marks where Simon's computer once sat.

They don't own a landline, and she has no way of contacting Assistant Commissioner Stirling or her team. She'll have to head out. Donning running gear, she pulls her wet hair into a ponytail and jams her keys and scattered possessions into her bag, before rushing to the front door. She pauses on the porch, notices the security camera that points to their entrance is gone. She runs back inside and down the hallway, opens the back door. The rear camera is also missing.

Bang. Bang. Bang.

She left the front door open, but someone's hammering on it anyway.

'Erica? Are you there?' a woman's voice demands.

She hurries back to the hallway to find Alex already inside, two of her surveillance officers trailing close behind.

'Thank God you're okay,' Alex says. Before Erica can respond, she starts talking to someone else via her body cam. 'Give me a minute. I'll check.'

Grasping Erica by the shoulders, she asks, 'Have you seen or heard from Senior Constable Murray? From Laura?'

Erica shakes her head as the two officers start searching the house.

'Wait!' Erica yells. 'Don't touch anything!' They all stop and turn to her for an explanation. 'Simon has skipped. He's taken my phone and laptop, along with all his belongings, computer and files.

'What colour scrubs does Simon wear?' Alex asks.

What kind of a stupid question –?

'Erica. What colour?'

'Black. Why do you ask?'

As the lift doors slide open to the executive floor, Assistant Commissioner Stirling is waiting for her, Alex and Ki, and Kate and Hannah. Without a word, he leads the group to Deputy Commissioner Jones's office.

Several people are already sitting around the table, including Leon, Bec Walraven and Erica's remaining surveillance officers

– Joel and George and Kyle and John. The DC waves them over, and Ki trots straight to Leon and sits beside him.

'You all know each other,' Jones says, 'so let's get to it. We don't have time to waste. Detective Jeffries, you have security camera footage showing Laura Murray being bundled into a car and abducted. Correct?'

Alex nods, but it's Leon who speaks, his words tumbling over each other in his haste. 'I checked the plate. It's fake. I've tried to call and trace Laura's phone, but no luck. Jess from my team is right now looking for other CCTV and traffic camera footage, but that will take some time.'

He points a remote control to a screen on the wall and hits play. 'This is the footage of the moment Laura was taken. You can see that one of the two men is wearing what looks like black hospital scrubs. I've already checked, and they're the type worn by interns at several Sydney hospitals, including Parramatta District. We believe this man may be Dr Simon Russell.'

Stirling turns to Erica. 'Is it him?'

Erica sits motionless, staring at the image on the screen before the Assistant Commissioner pushes again, 'Erica, is it him?'

'It could be.'

Alex adds, 'Dr Russell's cleared out, and we suspect he took Erica's devices with him.'

'Right,' DC Jones says, her face grim, 'what else do we know?'

Stirling jumps in. 'When our informant went missing, we suspected someone inside the taskforce was leaking information. Since then, we've been monitoring the activities of the various teams, looking for the mole. What we weren't aware of was that Mr Campbell here,' he gestures to Leon, 'already had suspicions about one of his staff and was pulling together the evidence he needed to bring it to our attention.'

Leon takes up the thread. 'I suspect Matt Baxter has been accessing my computer and files without authorisation, as well as potentially other taskforce information. Matt called in sick today.'

The DC raises her eyebrows. 'Not a coincidence, I suspect.'

'I passed Mr Campbell's material to Professional Standards,' Stirling says. 'As we speak, they are simultaneously checking Baxter's online activity, phone records and bank accounts, and paying him a personal visit. They'll let me know as soon as they have something concrete.'

'Good work, but our priority has to be finding Senior Constable Murray.' Jones turns to Bec Walraven. 'Can you spare some bodies to help the technical team source and review camera footage?'

'Of course.'

'Have you made any progress getting access to *TITAN*? Would that help find Laura?'

'No, not yet, Ma'am. But if Baxter is sharing information with one or more criminal groups, he may be using a *TITAN* device.'

'What's *TITAN*?' Leon asks.

'It's a new app we've been monitoring chatter about,' Bec explains. 'There's significant interest from different groups to get on board with it. It operates on the dark web and is being touted as a safe and secure platform for multi-group criminal communication and activity, including as a marketplace for drugs, firearms and other illegal transactions. We've been trying to get our hands on it, but it's been difficult. We believe users pay a hefty monthly fee to access and use the device. If they miss a payment, the device is disabled, and they lose connectivity. It's highly sophisticated and very secure.'

'Then you'd better get cracking, Bec,' Jones says. 'This suddenly got a lot more urgent.' Turning to Assistant Commissioner Stirling, she says, 'Sam, I want you to personally oversee the search for Senior Constable Murray. The rest of you - the assistant commissioner will allocate your priorities. Dismissed.'

The team files out, and Erica hovers in the corridor, waiting for Leon and Ki. When he emerges, she places her hand on his arm and pulls him aside. 'Can we talk?'

Leon wrenches his arm away before whispering back. 'Not now. There's no time. But you should know, if anything's happened to Laura, I don't think I'll ever forgive you.'

Chapter 43

Cain places new tape across Laura's mouth, turns off the light and leaves her in darkness.

She waits for the door to close and for the classical music to restart. When the sounds of moaning overlay the music, and she knows at least Karlie and Simon are busy, she begins testing the rope looped around her right hand. If she's right, it felt a little looser than the other bindings. She wriggles her wrist, moves it back and forth and pulls at the restraint, the rope burning her skin. It's slow work, and at any moment her captors could return. Grunting, she yanks with all her strength until her shoulder almost pops. But her cries of pain are muffled by her gag, and she continues to wriggle her right hand until, finally, she squeezes it free. Wincing, she rips the tape off her mouth.

She remembers the rock Karlie showed her. Is it still there? She can't feel the weight of it on the mattress. They wouldn't be so stupid as to leave it behind, would they? Her fingers slide across the satin sheet, searching anyway, but finding nothing.

Taking a deep breath, she swings her hips sideways and flings her right arm over. Her fingers scratch at the air, just short of the rope holding her left hand to the bed frame.

She tries again. No luck. This time she pulls harder against the rope binding her right leg, trying to create more leverage. Coarse fibres cut into her skin and blood trickles down her foot onto the sheets but still she keeps pushing.

In the background, the sound of lovemaking reaches a crescendo. Her time is almost up. Laura breathes in and out, blocking out the pain of the rope ripping into the flesh of her foot, swinging herself over with all her force. Her hand finally connects with the binding and she starts working on the knot.

Panting and with sweat dripping down her face, she pulls at the rope, worrying at it until ... *success*! Panicking that Karlie and Simon might be back any second, she reaches down and quickly unties her injured foot. She hears footsteps approaching as she fumbles with the sole remaining restraint, and she scrambles all the harder, swearing under her breath as she rushes to untie herself.

The knot releases, and, grabbing the discarded rope, she slides under the bed as the door opens and the light flickers on.

'What the hell?' Anderson blurts in confusion.

Without thinking, Laura darts out from under the bed and loops the rope around his knees, wrenching him toward her. Cain cries out as he's pulled off his feet but his shout is cut short by the sickening crack as his skull collides with the end of the jagged iron bed frame. He slumps to the ground, a crimson puddle spreading rapidly in all directions from his head.

Laura steps over the blood and checks the side of his neck for a pulse.

One down.

Chapter 44

It doesn't take long for Matt Baxter to be taken into custody. He's picked up at Sydney Airport carrying a fake passport, several thousand dollars in cash and three mobile phones, all of which are handed over to an excited Bec Walraven, who immediately starts examining them in the hope that one is a *TITAN* device. Matt himself, meanwhile, is delivered for questioning by the assistant commissioner, Erica, Alex and Professional Standards.

Keen as he is to sit in on the interrogation, Leon knows he's better off putting his particular skills to use looking for Laura – searching for camera footage that might tell them where they've taken her.

Together with Jess and two officers borrowed from the Cyber Unit, he starts mapping major roads connecting to the street where Laura was taken, seeking access to traffic camera footage in the hours leading up to and immediately after Laura was abducted. As the video starts coming in, he divides it up between them for analysis, throwing himself into the task.

Being active is the only way he can think of to keep his anxiety in check.

Headphones on, he scans video footage of cars from around 6:20 am, checking vehicles as they move along Heathcote Road, a busy thoroughfare connected to hers by two side streets.

There it is – the white SUV with the stolen plates.

He slows the footage down and tracks the vehicle before it turns onto New Illawarra Road. Then he loses it.

'Who's checking New Illawarra Road?' he asks his new team. 'I've got them turning onto it off Heathcote Road.'

He checks the timestamp and gives the others the window they need to be checking, and soon Jess yells, 'Got 'em!'

Leon rushes over and watches the screen as the vehicle moves along the road before turning off down a narrow side street. Then it's gone again.

'Find out what's on that road,' Leon tells her. 'There may be petrol stations or businesses that have cameras we can access.' Turning to the two cyber officers who've been allocated to him, he adds, 'Narrow your focus on the main roads leading off that street. I'll do the same.'

It's tedious work and Leon feels his anxiety rising when he realises they've been at it for almost two hours with no further breakthroughs. He's so focused on the task that he jumps at the tap on his shoulder. He twists in his seat to find Erica looking down at him.

'We've got news,' she whispers. 'Come to the briefing room and I'll fill you in.'

Leon leaps to his feet – Ki, who's been sitting quietly under the desk, is also up in an instant and the pair of them follow Erica out the door.

'Keep at it,' he calls to his team. 'I'll fill you in when I get back.'

He trails Erica down the corridor, knowing there is no way he'll last until the briefing room to find out what's happened. 'Do you know where she is?' he asks, his palms sweaty.

'Not yet, but we're close. Assistant Commissioner Stirling will fill you in.'

Stirling, Alex and Bec are all waiting in the briefing room, and Leon sits quickly, turning his gaze and attention at once to the senior officer. Stirling begins without delay.

'Your former colleague was initially … uncooperative,' he says, 'refusing to say anything without his lawyer. But when his legal representative arrived, we presented him with substantial evidence indicating his involvement with outside criminal agencies and told him we were busy tracing all the messages from his devices. His lawyer realised the way the wind was blowing and advised Baxter to share information, in the hope it will be considered in a positive light by prosecutors.'

'And what did he say?' Leon asks. He wants to cut to the chase and find out what they learned.

'You were right. He admitted he's been illegally accessing taskforce files and messages and sharing the information –

including surveillance arrangements – of who's on the taskforce and its progress. He's been dealing with two separate criminal groups, the 'Ndrangheta and the Scorpions, contacting both through his *TITAN* device, and helping them stay one step ahead of us. For a hefty fee, of course. He confessed to providing details about the police informant, Dan Garfield and removing the footage that would have confirmed the Scorpions were the ones who followed Dan to the gym.'

'And Laura?' Leon asks, holding his breath.

'That's when he clammed up,' Stirling begins, and a heavy weight settles on Leon's chest. 'However, we pointed out to his lawyer that once we crack the *TITAN* device, we'll have evidence to show Baxter was an accessory to the kidnapping of a police officer – an offence serious enough to put him behind bars for a long time. That convinced him to tell us what he knew, including several potential locations where missing women may have been taken, and where he's met both Cain Anderson and Dr Simon Russell. Laura could be at one of those locations.

'So, what are we doing here?' Leon demands, pushing back from his chair and causing Ki to jump to his feet.

Erica puts a hand on his arm and eases him back down. 'We've sent teams to each location. There are six houses spread out across western and southern Sydney, including Cain Anderson's residence at Heathcote. We'll know soon if the vehicle that took Laura is at any of them.

'We have to be very careful with this, Leon. If we spook her captors, God knows what they might do to her.'

Chapter 45

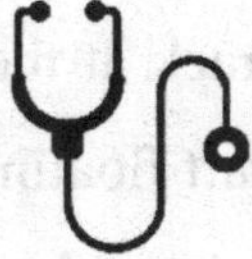

Karlie's nails rake down Simon's back, leaving deep scratches. Her panting grows louder and his own breathing quickens as she cries out in exultation as he explodes inside her. Falling onto his chest, she brushes her fingers across the rough stubble on his chin and lays her head against his heart.

'Now, wasn't that better than anything you did with Martin?'

'She meant nothing to me,' Simon replies. 'I've told you before, she was a job.' He lifts her chin and kisses her.

The scream and loud crash from the bedroom where Laura is tied up have them both leaping from the bed. Karlie pulls on her knickers and a crop top, then bends to rifle through a duffle bag on the floor. Simon drags on his underpants as she places her finger over her lips. She shows him the gun she's pulled from the bag and hands him a machete.

He follows her to Laura's room, passing the lounge on the way. There's no sign of Cain. Karlie points to the left, indicating he should approach the bedroom via the kitchen, while she pads through the lounge, taking the direct route.

Both arrive outside the bedroom without encountering anything alarming on the way. The door is closed and there's no light seeping through the crack at the bottom. All is quiet, save for the gentle sound of Mozart floating on the air.

Simon wonders if Cain is in there having a bit of fun with Laura. He knows the older man has an unhealthy fixation with young women. Perhaps this drama is all for nothing, but when he glances at Karlie, her expression tells him this is no false alarm.

Machete raised, Simon turns the knob; he eases the door open and steps through it, his left hand searching for the light switch.

Something whips around his neck, and he drops his weapon, the machete clattering to the ground. Gagging, he's dragged backwards, away from Karlie, and his feet slip on something wet and slick, sending him to his knees and tightening whatever is looped around his neck.

'Drop the gun or he's dead!' Laura barks, and Simon splutters as she yanks harder on the rope.

Karlie sneers and aims her gun at Laura's head. 'You don't have the guts.'

'Yeah? Tell that to Cain,' Laura says, motioning to his lifeless form in the pool of blood. Simon gasps for air as Laura twists the rope, keeping him in front of her as a human shield.

'Karlie …' he pants. 'Help me.'

The seconds stretch out as he struggles to breathe.

Karlie edges away from the bloody puddle oozing across the floor toward her. The red, expanding pool flashes Simon's oxygen-starved brain to the 1960s horror movie *The Blob*.

Karlie still has the upper hand. She has the gun. Simon knows Laura is bound by morals and rules. Karlie isn't. But he also knows that if you back someone into a corner, give them nothing to lose, they'll do anything to save themselves.

'Don't you want to know how I got free?' Laura teases.

'Cain obviously stuffed up the knots,' Karlie says, maintaining her aim. 'He was becoming a liability. You've done me a favour.'

'Oh, it wasn't Cain,' Laura says. 'It was *Loverboy* here.'

'No,' Simon croaks. 'That's not true.'

Karlie's eyes narrow and suddenly the anger that's been simmering just below the surface explodes. 'Bullshit!'

Laura laughs. 'When he checked on me, after I came to, he loosened the knot on my right hand. Not too much, but enough. He gave me a chance. I took it.'

'No … Karlie,' Simon splutters. 'Don't … believe her.'

Karlie's head snaps to the side as the front door crashes in. They've found them.

'NO!' Karlie screams, and, snarling, she raises her gun, fires twice.

Laura falls to the floor beneath him and Simon gulps like a beached fish as the pressure is released from his neck.

Chapter 46

The convoy parks a block away and Erica gathers with her team for final instructions. The six surveillance officers who have worked side by side on Taskforce Lacuna are joined by members of the Tactical Operations Unit, their faces are grim as they check their weapons.

When Leon confirms that they're successfully jamming the property's security cameras, and they know that teams are in place and ready to go at the other addresses provided by Matt Baxter, Stirling reiterates each team's role.

Alex, Erica and Ki will go in with seven of the highly trained officers while three more will take up positions at the back of the house, along with Erica's surveillance officers.

Everyone is kitted up and wearing bulletproof vests. Even Ki, who is decked out in a special protective dog vest. Sniffing the ground, he picks up his handler's scent and whines, looking up at Erica, eager to go.

'It's okay, boy,' she says. 'We'll find her.'

Leon's voice crackles in the earpiece of her tactical headset. 'Be careful, all of you. And please, bring her home.'

'We will. I promise,' Erica replies, picturing him at his desk, watching the action through her body camera.

'All right, everyone, let's move,' Stirling announces, and the teams move off. Ki races to the lead, Erica sprinting to keep up, the tactical officers on her heels. Ki takes them along the street and to the front yard of the nondescript, brown-brick 1980s home, where Erica has to pull him back to allow the tactical officers access to the front door.

'On one,' the assistant commissioner says, synchronising the front- and rear-door entries. 'Three. Two. One.'

Two officers swing a heavy metal ram into the front door, shaking it from its hinges before it crashes to the ground.

Two gunshots echo from inside the house, and Ki pulls free of Erica, ducking around the specialist tactical men and racing towards the source of the sounds.

Erica sprints after him, arriving in time to witness the dog launching himself at a woman with a gun. The woman staggers as Ki's full weight slams into her, but rolls away, throwing the dog into the wall.

Ki lands with a sickening crunch. He doesn't move.

Spinning around, the woman turns the gun on Erica.

It's like the world is moving at half speed. The cries of the tactical officers are drowned out by the sound of Erica's heart drumming in her ears. As the woman's gun raises to point at her,

Erica's own firearm comes up, steady and smooth, as she's been trained.

Her finger squeezes the trigger, and the bullet bursts from her weapon.

The woman drops, a fine spray of blood from the fatal shot clouding the air.

'Erica? Erica. Are you all right?'

It takes a moment for her to register the insistent voice from her comms unit. 'Fine. Fine. I'm okay,' she mutters into her headset microphone, unable to take her eyes off the woman sprawled before her.

'Officer down, officer down!'

The panicked call echoes through the house.

'No, no, no,' the voice cries in her earpiece.

Leon.

She hurries in the direction of the shouting, turns into a small bedroom. Three people lie motionless on the floor.

One is Cain Anderson. He's surrounded by blood. His head caved in. Her heart falters as she identifies the second.

Two members of the Tactical Operations Unit are rolling Simon's lifeless form off Laura, who is coughing and spluttering from the crushing weight of his body. She is smeared in blood, with cuts to her hands and feet, but most of the gore has come from the bullet wounds. One shot nicked her ear, but it was the second, which took Simon in the head, that is responsible for most of the mess on her.

Leon is shouting in Erica's ear, but she doesn't hear him. All she can focus on is Laura.

'Erica. You came,' Laura pants as the officers lift her from the floor.

Erica takes off her jacket, placing it around her friend and the two embrace.

'I'm sorry,' Laura stutters. She's shivering as shock sets in. 'I didn't want anyone to die.'

'You had to save yourself,' Erica says.

'I think he tried to help me in the end,' Laura stutters. 'Loosened one of the knots holding me. That's how I got free. And I used that …' Laura shudders and her words falter. 'I used that to turn her against him.'

'Laura, I'm so sorry,' Erica whispers. 'You tried to warn me. But I was so happy in my cocoon, I didn't want to believe it. Couldn't believe it.' Her voice breaks as she pulls her friend close. 'Oh, my God. I could have saved you from this.'

'You did save me,' Laura murmurs, before Assistant Commissioner Stirling steps forward, wraps a blanket around her and shepherds her to a waiting medical team.

Chapter 47

Laura doesn't utter a word on the drive home from the hospital, instead staring out the window at the passing traffic. Her right arm is in a sling, her right foot heavily bandaged and her ear taped up. The doctors have discharged her with painkillers, antibiotics and clean bandages but she'll need to see her GP for follow-up treatment.

Her physical injuries will heal. Erica is more concerned about her mental load.

'Have you let your mum and dad know what's happened?' she asks as they pull up to the curb outside Laura's house.

'Tomorrow,' Laura replies, still gazing out the window. 'I need to rest tonight.'

'Of course.' Erica turns off the engine. 'You must be starving. Leon's getting pizza and some of my clothes. We're both going to stay with you for a while. If that's okay?'

'You don't have to babysit me, Erica.' Laura's voice is short and sharp, her face flushed.

Erica doesn't react. Her friend is in pain; she needs to express that. 'I know, but I want to. At least for a few days, to give you a hand while you recover.'

She gets out of the car and jogs around to the passenger side to get the door. Laura glares at her, and Erica steps back as she fumbles with the door and Laura clambers out. She moves slowly – every step must be agony.

Erica matches her stride as they shuffle to her front door. Laura digs out her keys one-handed, drops them; Erica picks them up, opens the door and waits for her to go in first. Laura hobbles to the lounge room and lowers herself onto the couch with a deep sigh.

'Leon will be here soon with the food,' Erica says. 'Do you want a cup of tea, or would you like to watch some TV, or listen to music? I can run you a bath or help you in the shower. The doctor said to try and avoid getting your foot wet but I'm sure we can manage it.'

'Tea. A cup of tea … please.'

Erica finds a stash of herbal teas, a teapot and some cups and waits for the peppermint leaves to steep. Searching in the cupboards, she takes out a circular tray, and finds some Tim Tams in the fridge. Leon arrives as she's setting the tray on the coffee table, his arms full of pizzas and garlic bread. Erica waves him to the kitchen; they place the food onto plates and return to the lounge room.

'Hey, how are you feeling?' Leon kisses Laura on the cheek and sits beside her. She shrugs. 'I got a pepperoni and a tandoori chicken,' he goes on, and Laura picks up a piece without looking at it. She starts nibbling at the edges, but her attempt is half-hearted at best.

'You don't have to eat it if you don't want to,' Erica says. 'I can put it in the fridge for tomorrow. Pizza's always better the next day anyway.'

Laura drops the slice onto her plate. Erica stares at Leon, her eyes wide, beseeching him to help.

'Where's Ki?' Laura asks, her voice breaking. 'He's gone, isn't he? They came back and took care of him, didn't they? Just tell me. I need to know.'

Erica struggles to remain composed in the face of her friend's obvious distress. 'We found him at your place when we went to check on you. He was fine but …' Erica glances at Leon. He nods; she has to be told sometime. 'He got injured today when we came for you. He's staying overnight at the vet. They're doing x-rays to check for any breaks but they hope he's only pulled some ligaments. If that's the case, he will heal in a few weeks. You can visit him tomorrow if you want.'

Laura absorbs the news for a moment, then bursts into tears. Leon takes her in his arms, her body heaving as she sobs into his chest.

'It'll be all right,' he murmurs, cradling her and caressing her face.

As Leon drags a box of tissues from the coffee table to his lap and wipes the tears from Laura's face, Erica gathers the food and retreats to the kitchen, where she watches in silence. At last, the crying subsides and Laura pulls back from her boyfriend.

'I'm sorry. I didn't mean to lose it on you.'

'No apology needed,' Leon responds. 'I'm here for you. Now, how about you have some tea and I'll get your bed ready?'

He starts to rise from the lounge, but Laura drags him back down. 'Can you stay with me. Hold me. I don't think I can sleep. I don't want to dream.'

Erica fights to keep her own tears in check as Leon replies, his voice shaky. 'Of course I'll hold you. Forever … even longer.'

Laura's laugh is light and soft in response.

And out of nowhere, Erica is ambushed by thoughts of Simon. He used to hold her like that.

But it was all a lie.

She chokes down the lump rising in her throat, sadness surging into anger when she thinks about what could have happened to Laura. She is Erica's priority now. Simon can't hurt them anymore.

She fetches a pillow and blankets, and Laura stretches out on the lounge, laying her head in Leon's lap as she struggles to stay awake. Her eyes close and her breathing slows.

Erica crouches beside them and whispers, 'I think it's best if I leave you two alone. Thanks for getting my bag but I'll go home. If you need me, call. Anytime.'

Leon nods and Erica heads for the front door. Pausing at the entrance, she turns. Leon is stroking Laura's hair, his body rising and falling with silent tears.

Chapter 48

Taking a deep breath, his nostrils flaring, he dials her number.

Erica picks up on the second ring. 'Leon, is everything okay?'

'Laura's doing alright but I've been called back to the office. I don't want to go, but they need me. Can you come over and look after her, while I'm at work?'

'Of course. I'll get dressed. Be right there.'

'Thanks,' the word struggles from his lips and he hangs up.

By the time Erica arrives, Laura has had a shower and is nibbling at some toast at the kitchen bench.

He leans in and whispers in her ear that he loves her before kissing her cheek, grabbing his bag, nodding at Erica and striding out the door.

At different points on the drive to headquarters he's almost turned around. He wants to be with her, support her, but he's also determined to do his bit to bring all those involved in the trafficking ring to justice. He owes her that.

This morning, he swallowed his resentment of the woman he once admired, not wanting to upset Laura during her recovery, but whenever he thinks about what could have been, his anger is like a sore that he keeps picking at, a wound that won't heal.

But it's nothing compared to the fury that courses through him when he thinks of his former team member, Matt.

Jess greets him with an awkward hug. She's not a touchy-feely person, so Leon recognises how concerned she must be for Laura and for him.

He logs in, checks his messages and then logs off and joins Jess at the morning briefing with the assistant commissioner, Alex and the surveillance teams.

He and Jess are on their own, with all of Bec's crew working non-stop on the *TITAN* device. Their job is to compile all the footage from the taskforce for use as evidence. There are mountains of it and it will take several days to complete.

After the briefing, he and Jess return to their area. He stares at the two empty workstations before a tentative hand on his arm brings him back to the present.

'I know you need caffeine; do you want to go to Stefanos and grab a coffee before we start?' Jess asks, her eyes wide and sad.

'No, I'll just get an instant from the kitchen, but thanks for the offer. I want to get this done as soon as possible.'

Jess nods and they divvy up the work between them. Heads down, they get to it. Before long, Jess is telling him she's taking her lunch break.

A few minutes later, Alex calls him to her office.

'How's Laura doing?' she asks, leaning across the desk with her chin in her hands.

'It will take a while, but she's strong. Stronger than even she realises.'

'Please tell her we are all thinking about her. And now, how are you going?'

'Fine. I'm okay.'

Alex raises her eyebrows and continues to stare at him across the table.

'Honestly. I just want to do what I can here, then look after her,' he replies to the question that wasn't spoken.

Alex rises, placing her hand on her monitor, 'By the way, you were right about Matt Baxter; he was a much better cyber-criminal than we gave him credit for, and your tip-off was the break we needed. You look like you need a few minutes to yourself. You're welcome to hang out in my office for a while,' she says as she swings her monitor around, the screen displaying a frame of the video of the interview with Matt, before closing the door behind her.

Leon grabs her mouse and clicks play.

'Mr Baxter, we know you have some excellent IT skills, otherwise you wouldn't have been able to hack into our systems without detection for so long, but you must realise that Dr Walraven here,' Alex gestures toward Bec, who's sitting impassive and silent beside her, 'is one of the best in the business. She and her team will crack this device—sooner rather than later. So, why don't you cooperate and give us access now. Save everyone some time.'

'I need a moment to consult with my client,' Matt's lawyer says and Alex and Bec nod and leave the room. Leon knows they're watching on as the video shows Matt and his lawyer having an animated, whispered conversation. After three minutes of hushed arguing, Matt resolutely shakes his head. His lawyer huffs in frustration before opening the door and telling them they're ready to resume the interview.

Alex and Bec take their seats opposite the pair.

'Mr Baxter says he can't remember the passwords or how to access the device,' the lawyer says through gritted teeth.

'Hmm … a sudden case of amnesia, hey?' Alex teases. 'Well, I'll just make a note of this in my report. The Director of Public Prosecutions will be most interested.'

Alex turns to her colleague, 'So, Dr Walraven. It's over to you. How long do you need?'

'We've already made excellent progress. My team should have it cracked in a couple of hours,' Bec says, all the while staring directly at Matt, who is now squirming in his chair.

'Well, then, seems like we've got all we need for now. It's a pity you didn't want to cooperate and give us access; it might have made a big difference ...' She's cut off by Matt, who's looking more and more uncomfortable.

'I gave you the locations, remember? I have helped,' his voice is almost pleading.

Alex pushes back her chair and gathers a folder into her arms as she prepares to end the interview. 'Oh yes. And I'm sure the DPP will consider that but helping us with *TITAN*—that's a whole new ball game.'

'What about my request for witness protection? I'll tell you if you can get me in. You were going to do it for Dan Garfield, surely you can do it for me? Otherwise, I can't help you,' Matt blurts before his lawyer can stop him.

'So, you *do* remember. This short-term memory loss works in funny ways, doesn't it?' Alex scoffs.

'My client has said he will consider cooperating but only if you can guarantee him protection. He has nothing more to say.'

The interview is halted while Alex consults with Assistant Commissioner Stirling and the DC. It resumes an hour later but when Alex returns to the interview room, she's alone. Matt glances back at the door when Alex takes her seat.

'Dr Walraven is a little busy at the moment, she's very close to cracking *TITAN*,' Alex says in response. 'So, Mr Baxter, the commissioner is considering your request, but you need to understand it's time-limited. As soon as the Cyber Intelligence Unit accesses the app, witness protection is off the table.'

Matt's lawyer leans over and whispers in his ear as Alex takes out her phone and taps out a message, seemingly oblivious to the urgent conversation across the table.

Running his fingers through his hair and his eyes darting from his lawyer to Alex, Matt finally relents and provides passwords and details on how they can access *TITAN*.

After watching the video, his respect for Alex and Bec deepens. Without access to *TITAN*, they wouldn't have a hope of tracking the entire trafficking network. Now they have the upper hand.

Once they got in, Bec and her team went all-out to download messages and data on the app.

'We're very lucky our bluff worked,' Bec reports at an operational briefing with the DC, Stirling, Alex and Leon that afternoon. 'It would have potentially taken days, if not much longer, to crack it. I've never come across anything as complex as this before.'

'I've let my counterparts in the AFP and state forces know we're snooping around on the app, but it's a top-secret operation. Highly restricted "need to know", but what's next?' the DC asks, turning to Bec.

'I have a plan. If it works, it will put us in control. I'm crafting what will appear to be a mandatory system update for the platform, but it will contain a trojan. As soon as they install it, we will be able to monitor everything the users say to each other.'

'Will it work?' the DC asks.

'I'm pretty confident it will. It's actually based on highly successful trojans used by cyber criminals themselves. My team are testing it now. It won't be long before we're ready to deploy it,' Bec responds, and Leon is in awe of her calm demeanour. She could be reciting a shopping list, not describing a major operational breakthrough.

'Brilliant,' the DC responds and grins broadly, 'if we pull this off, it will be a game changer. Now, where are we at with the bikie Merlin?'

Stirling responds, 'We've been tailing him. He's been lying low at the Scorpions clubhouse. We have an arrest and search warrant but we're waiting for him to move. We don't want to charge in and have a shootout with him and his bikie mates or move too soon and alert key players to our other activities.'

The DC nods, 'Sensible. But I want him in custody as soon as possible …'

'I'm sorry to interrupt, ma'am, but we could send him a message on *TITAN*, lure him somewhere where we can arrest him,' Bec suggests.

'Would he take the bait?' Stirling asks.

'He met Cain Anderson at The Star Tavern before. What if we pretend that Anderson wants to meet with him again at the same place? He doesn't know Anderson is dead, does he?' Leon asks, and the officers in the room nod.

'It might work, sir, but we should do it as soon as we can. The longer we wait, the more chance they will realise something isn't right,' Alex says to the assistant commissioner.

'Agreed, but once we take Merlin down, they'll know for sure we're onto them, especially if we use *TITAN* to get to him. Keep watching him, and as soon as Bec and the team upload the trojan and everyone is ready, we move,' the DC says.

The following day, Leon and Alex, together with five tactical officers, are in a plain white van parked around the corner from the tavern. Special operations officers are already inside waiting for Merlin when the rumble of a motorcycle engine grows louder.

On her headset, Alex alerts the officers inside.

The pinhole cameras in their jackets show the pub is almost deserted except for them and a woman in her fifties who has the skinny, weathered look of a junkie. She's leaning across the bar chatting to the publican.

Leon watches on as the two officers start shouting before pushing each other in the chest.

'Oi, stop that. If you wanna fight, take it outside,' the gruff voice of the barman is audible over the hidden microphones.

He keeps watching as the argument escalates. He hears a stool being thrown to the ground before the face of the barman comes into view. He steps between the two men, spit flying out of his mouth as he yells at them to get out.

On the screen, he watches the two officers, still swearing and jostling with each other, push through the front doors into the cold night air.

Alex and her backup team leap out of the van, sprinting toward the tavern, and Leon listens as she issues instructions through her headset.

The camera view from the two officers, still pretending to argue with each other, swings around to show Merlin getting off his bike.

Leon watches the different feeds – the two officers moving toward Merlin and the bumpy feed of Alex and her team as they sprint toward the bikie.

Merlin spins around, a confused look on his face, as the two men grab him and twist his arms behind his back before thrusting him to the ground and cuffing him. Panting, Alex stands over Merlin as they lift him up. 'Nicholas Parelli, you are under arrest …'

Leon leans into the screen, watching the bikie as he laughs in Alex's face, 'What for, sweetheart? I'm just here to have a beer. Is that a crime?'

Alex ignores his taunt as he is led away.

The night of Merlin's arrest, raids are conducted across Australia, New Zealand, Asia and Europe, leading to multiple arrests. When the special operations teams charged the other properties around Sydney, they discovered Tori, Sophie and

Siobhan, who are receiving medical treatment and being interviewed about their abduction.

Of Meg and Cassie, there is no sign, but hope remains.

In New South Wales alone, the monitoring of messaging across the app helped to thwart five murder plots and shut down numerous drug labs. This resulted in the seizure of more than 30 firearms and other weapons, around $10 million in cash and crypto currency, jewellery and several luxury cars. Also, the confiscation of significant quantities of cocaine, cannabis and MDMA, plus almost a tonne of black-market cigarettes and vapes.

The takeover of *TITAN* caused maximum damage to organised crime in Australia and overseas, with the AFP and their international partners across Asia and Europe using the information to unravel a complex network of criminal associations. The AFP is working with overseas agencies to help them track down the remaining missing women, Meg and Cassie.

Alex informed him that Richard Ryan, the detective originally involved with the taskforce who was sidelined after suffering a major stroke, recovered enough to share with her that he'd pulled up Ally Webster's file because, even though there was a significant time lapse between her disappearance and the other women, he felt there were also many similarities. Such as the unexpected nature of her disappearance, when Ally was relatively happy in her life and had no reason to leave, and that it occurred in suburban Sydney. He'd intended to investigate further but was hospitalised.

Meanwhile, a defiant Merlin refuses to answer any questions or cooperate in any way. Search teams with cadaver dogs are combing bushland close to each of the properties Baxter revealed under interrogation.

So far, Ally Webster's remains and the rest of Dan Garfield's body have not been found.

After a long, late night supporting the operation to arrest Merlin, Leon climbs into bed beside Laura. She stirs almost instantly.

'You're home. You look tired,' she says as she rubs the creases around his eyes.

'I'm fine,' he murmurs, 'go back to sleep.'

She kisses him before turning and curling herself against his body.

Later, he calms her when the bad dreams return.

Chapter 49

For Laura, the next two weeks pass in a blur. She spends a full day being interviewed and debriefed on the events leading up to her kidnapping, the deaths of Cain Anderson and Dr Simon Russell, her rescue, and the shooting of Karlie Wilson. She's informed by Assistant Commissioner Stirling that there will be an inquest into the deaths of the criminals and the taskforce's role in them, and in the meantime, she is to consider herself on sick leave. Initially, there will be six weeks while her body heals, but that could be extended on review by Stirling, based on a recommendation by an operational psychologist about when she'll be ready to don the uniform again.

Stirling, who has taken over control of Erica's teams on Taskforce Lacuna has insisted on a face-to-face, weekly wellbeing check with Laura. Ki takes up his usual position at her feet as the senior officer questions her about her recovery.

'I'm healing well. The doctor says I should be out of the sling in a couple of weeks and then I'll start physio to build the muscles back up.'

'But how are you *feeling*, Murray?'

'The psych sessions are helping a lot,' Laura bravely replies as Stirling consults a piece of paper in front of him.

Looking up, he points to a plaque on the wall, 'See that? It's a commendation from the Police Commissioner and Premier for my role in ending a hostage situation 10 years ago. You would have heard about it. It was all over the news at the time. The father had a history of domestic violence and serious mental health issues. His wife left him, but he tracked her down and killed her. He took the kids, aged only 4 and 6 and held them hostage. For 48 hours, we tried to convince him to let them go, but he wouldn't listen. He was becoming more and more unstable. In the end, we stormed the house. He had a gun pointed at the heads of his children, who were tied to a chair in front of him. I had no choice. I took his life.'

He turns back to Laura, whose face has paled as she absorbs what her senior officer has shared. 'We are here to protect and serve. Sometimes we have to make hard decisions, life and death decisions, but we do what no one else can. That's what we're trained for. What you've trained for. You had no choice either.'

Her tears are falling freely now and Stirling hands over tissues. Wiping her eyes, she asks, 'How long did it take for you, sir, to get over it … taking someone's life?'

'It gets easier over time,' he replies, 'as it will for you too.'

Laura nods and the assistant commissioner reads from the psychologist's report in front of him, giving her time to regain her composure. 'I understand you want to do your next few sessions over video conference with the psychologist. You want to visit your family?'

'Yes. The psych said it would be okay and a good idea for me to spend time with my family for a while. I haven't told them what really happened. I want to do that in person, but without any sensitive operational details, of course.'

'I understand. Family is important. Just make sure you don't skip the sessions. I'll know,' he says, tapping the paper in front of him.

Laura nods, then swallows hard. 'Leon – Mr Campbell – has struggled to juggle his heavy workload and look after me, but can you spare him, sir, for a couple of weeks? To come with me? It would mean a lot, and to be honest, he needs some time off too, but he'll never ask.'

'We'll work something out. I'll talk to Mr Campbell.'

'Thank you, sir.'

'Right. Let's keep this day and time and do our weekly check-in over the phone while you're away. And keep up the psych appointments. Take care, Murray.'

'Thank you, sir. I will.'

Erica confided to her that she was strongly encouraged to take leave by Stirling and DC Jones and has also been attending sessions with the police psychologist. She is under investigation by Professional Standards because of her intimate relationship with Simon.

She's pacing in Laura's tiny lounge room, fretting about the future. 'I get it. They're questioning how I could be fooled by someone who was involved with these groups and not realise?'

'Erica, you can't blame yourself ...' Laura tries to reply but is cut off.

'I fell for the dream, Laura. For the relationship with the handsome, good doctor. I was sucked in by the nice guy routine. But it was all a lie. You tried to tell me ...' her voice fades off as Leon abruptly rises from the couch and strides to the kitchen, mumbling something about making Laura a sandwich.

Erica takes the spot he just vacated next to Laura. Leaning in, she whispers, 'He's so angry. I don't think he'll ever forgive me. But that's okay, I don't know if I'll ever forgive myself.'

Laura glances at the loud noise of clanking cutlery and plates echoing from the kitchen. 'He'll come around. Give him time.' Reaching out with her free hand, she touches Erica's arm. 'If you hadn't taken care of Karlie, I don't know how I'd cope. I'd always be thinking she'd try again. For me, there's nothing to forgive. Will you be okay while we're away?'

'I'll be fine. Don't worry about me,' Erica reassures her.

Leon is in the office, wrapping up loose ends before taking leave to be with Laura and visit their families. Erica has been struggling with a recurring stomach flu and Laura finally convinced her to go to the doctor.

When she returned from her appointment, Erica said they both needed some vitamin D, whisking Laura away for a picnic lunch by the river. As Erica spreads a blanket on the grass under a gum tree and starts unpacking the food she's brought along, Laura closes her eyes and lets the noise of the city fade away. The sounds of a young magpie squawking for a meal drown them out. She opens her eyes and watches the mother bird – not much bigger than the chick – feeding it.

'Have you ever wanted to be a parent?' Erica asks, also observing the older magpie shoving food down the overgrown chick's beak.

'One day,' Laura replies. 'To be honest, I haven't thought about it much. What about you?'

'I always wanted a career first,' Erica says. She flinches slightly as she goes on. 'Simon and I never talked about it. We were enjoying just being together, and it was too soon to try for a baby. At least I thought so.'

'What are you trying to say?' Laura asks, although she's certain she already knows.

'I'm pregnant.'

Laura stares. Surely not. God wouldn't do this to someone like Erica, wouldn't put her in such an awful position.

Erica laughs at the shock on Laura's face. 'It's ironic really. Me, a copper, knocked up by my now-dead ex-partner, who turned out to be working with the criminals I was chasing. You couldn't make this up.'

Laura takes her friend's hand. 'That's a lot.' It's all she can think of to say, and it sets Erica off laughing again, until the tears wash away her humour.

'What am I going to do?' she sobs.

'How far along are you?'

'About seven weeks. My doctor gave me a pack of information to read. About my choices. I know you're a spiritual person, so I understand if you don't want to talk about that.'

'I was brought up Catholic but I have my own values,' Laura answers. 'I don't agree with everything the church says or does. I stopped going to mass when I left home because I don't believe I need to be in a church to be connected to God or to prove that I'm a good person. I believe in treating people the way you want to be treated. In the end, the choice is yours and yours alone. Whatever you do, I'm your friend; I'll understand and stand by you.'

Erica rests her head on her shoulder as Laura pats her back until the tears stop, the song of the magpies filling their ears. With everything Karlie and Simon have destroyed, this she knows, is one thing they could never tear down.

Chapter 50

The information on the website is clear and concise. It's written with sensitivity but succinctly outlines the facts about every step of the process and all the risks involved.

Erica's read it so many times she can almost recite the words. But with Laura and Leon visiting their family at the coast, this is still the first time she's had to think clearly. Laura has been nothing but supportive, stressing she'll stand by Erica and help in any way she can, but what Erica has really needed is space to decide.

And now that's what she's going to do.

Pulling her top up over her stomach, she runs her hands over her toned and flat tummy. It's surreal that there is a life growing inside her. Yes, she's always wanted to be a mum one day, but she never pictured it would be like this. She hasn't told her family, difficult as it has been to hide it from her parents; they'd want to be with her. And she certainly hasn't mentioned it to anyone at work. Laura has kept her word by not telling a soul, not even Leon.

The clock is ticking.

Her phone rings and she picks it up, assuming it's Laura checking in on her. She's surprised when she realises it's her mother's number. They only spoke last night.

'Hi Mum, what's up?'

Silence. Then sobbing.

'Mum,' Erica says, her voice sharp, heart suddenly racing. 'Are you all right? What's happened? Where's Dad?'

It's not her mother but her father who answers, the echo on the line sounding like he has her on speaker.

'It's your grandfather' he says, voice trembling. 'He's … gone. Heart attack. This morning. There was nothing the paramedics could do.'

'Oh, my God,' Erica whispers. She pictures the tough but gentle man who has been an inspiration to her all her life and the reason she became a police officer. 'He wasn't even sick. Was he?'

'The doctors say he was probably unwell for a while but hid it from us. Most likely there had been symptoms, but he didn't tell anyone.'

Her mother's voice cuts in. 'Erica, he made you executor of his will.'

'He did?'

'There's more,' her father continues. 'He left a letter, sealed and addressed to you. It says it's to be opened only by you, and only after his funeral.'

In the background, Erica's mother starts sobbing again. 'Sweetheart, can you come home? Please? To help? Dad – your granddad – he was so organised. He had a funeral plan, and everything is paid for, and there are clear instructions about what he wants, but I … I can't do it.'

'Of course. Don't worry, Mum, I'll sort it out.'

'Thank you, darling,' her mother says, and then her father is back on the line.

'Thank you, Rici', he says, using her childhood nickname. 'We knew this would happen sometime, but your grandfather was still so active. And after losing your grandmother not that long ago, it's … it's a lot for your mum to process.'

Erica brushes the tears from her face. 'I get it, Dad. It's okay. I'll message you later, but I'll be there sometime in the morning.'

Then she drops the phone to her lap before placing her head in her hands and shaking with the force of her grief.

Erica straightens her uniform and faces the people who've come to pay their respects to her grandfather, Bill Matthews. It's standing room only, with many of the Cowra community in attendance. Instead of black, everyone who isn't a police officer is dressed in varying shades of green, her grandfather's favourite colour.

In the instructions he left for his funeral, her grandfather had said he didn't want people to be sad; he wanted his service to be full of colour and a celebration of his life. Instead of flowers, he asked for donations to the Cancer Council and Beyond Blue, in recognition of the disease that took his wife from him and the mental health struggles that his only son, Erica's Uncle Jim, couldn't overcome.

Her mother and father sit in the front row, staring at her. She still hasn't told them about the baby but coming home and dealing with this has made her realise how precious life is.

Unfolding sheaves of paper and pressing them flat on the lectern, she takes a deep breath and begins.

'Bill Matthews, my grandfather, served in the NSW Police for almost 40 years. He started as a Constable in Cowra and was posted across regional NSW. During his time in the force, he earned a reputation as a fair but firm officer, instilling pride and respect in the uniform and a desire to help the community in all who served with him. His last post was as an instructor at the training academy, where he shaped the officers of the future.

'I remember watching him as a little girl pressing his uniform and polishing his shoes. He'd reinforce what an honour it was to wear the badge. How serious and what a privilege it is to hold a position of authority and trust. What it meant to him to serve and protect his community. I never forgot that, and it was my grandfather's values and career that inspired me to join the force too.

'He never brought the pressure of the job, any problems, home with him. Or if he did, it never showed. After a few years in the force and struggling with some of the things I was witnessing on the job, I asked him how he'd managed it. He said, "Rici, the job is important, and when you're on the clock, you give it you're all. But family is more important. When you take that uniform off, you have to mentally leave your work on the hanger."

'After he retired at 65, having achieved the rank of superintendent, my grandfather returned to the place and town that he always called home. Cowra.

'But Bill was also a loving father, to my mum, Helen, and my Uncle Jim. He never recovered from losing my uncle, who suffered from serious mental health issues and sadly took his own life. He remained a devoted husband of more than 60 years to my grandmother, Beryl and was, of course, a loving grandfather to me and my brother, Joseph, who couldn't be here but is watching live from London. Bill was a keen golfer and competitive bridge player and could often be found with his head in a sudoku puzzle.'

Erica grins before continuing, 'He also had a wicked sense of humour and loved playing pranks on his colleagues and family. He enjoyed baking and would often make cakes and treats for his grandkids. One day, he baked chocolate chip cupcakes and inserted hot chilli paste directly into two of them, intending to give them to my brother and me. But my grandmother was the one who got them out of the oven and put them on the plate, so he lost track of which ones were which. In the end, he got one of the spicy cupcakes himself and, laughing, his eyes watering from the heat, confessed to what he'd done.'

The congregation laughs and Erica continues, 'I'm sure you all have stories you can share about Bill. He asked that instead of crying, you have a beer and swap yarns about his life, the good, the bad and the funny. And you are all invited to the bowling club after the service to do just that.

'My grandfather was an extraordinary human being. Someone who was a ferocious and loyal friend, smart and funny, and a role model for many, including me. He left only one other request for his service – that I share the following passage with you all.'

Keeping her tears in check and her back straight, she reads, 'There is a time for everything, and a season for every activity under the heavens: a time to be born and a time to die.'

Erica returns to her seat and as the curtains close on her grandfather's coffin, the sound of bagpipes fills the chapel.

That evening, after an exhausting day, Erica sits on the bed in her old room and opens the letter he left her. She reads and rereads it before letting the pages flutter to the floor.

Chapter 51

Huddled under an umbrella with Leon and Ki by her side, Laura watches the rain drip down the names etched in the rock, a tribute to the people whose lives Gary ripped away. She replaces the withered roses under the memorial with a fresh bouquet of yellow sunflowers, then speaks to her lost friends: Joanna's brothers, Benny and Jordy.

'Hey boys, I'm sorry it's been so long since I visited last,' she whispers to the stone as she traces her fingers across its rough surface. 'Your sister is doing really well. She's a mum to Katie and now to little Arthur Jordan and Hudson Benjamin. The twins are troublemakers, just like their uncles.' She smiles sadly. 'We miss you, all of us,'

The wind picks up and drives rain into their faces as they walk back to the car. 'Joanna told me the old pub is quite trendy now,' Laura says as Leon holds the umbrella over her and helps her into the passenger seat. With her arm still in a sling for a little longer, Leon's declared himself her official chauffeur. 'They've upgraded the beer garden and bistro and they even stock dog beers.'

'Sounds good,' Leon says. 'Stop there after the farm?'

'Let's.'

Laura directs him through the small town of Wallaby Rock to the housing development that was once the site of her family farm. A black metal sign attached to one of two stone pillars that mark the entrance tells them they've entered The Old Dairy Estate, and Laura wipes away a tear as she realises the main road is Murray Drive.

New streets peel this way and that across what used to be paddocks like scars on the landscape and Laura points out where the farmhouse and milking sheds used to stand. Homes and townhouses are crammed onto modest-sized blocks. Earlier in the day, chatting with a builder, she'd learned the second stage of construction has started, with demand outstripping supply. The developer has even bought out neighbouring farms to make this one of the largest new housing estates in the area.

The estate eats into cleared bushland Laura loved to roam as a child, and she asks Leon to park at the last vacant block beside it. Getting out of the car, she leads the way, Leon and Ki close behind and they are soon in the cover of the trees.

Once she's under the canopy, it feels like she's never been away, and she weaves her way through the scrub until she comes to a cliff. Standing back, she takes in the view of the gorge and river below, just like she had when she was young.

'Wow, Laura, this is so beautiful. Is this where you used to hang out?'

'Yeah. This is my place,' Laura replies as she moves closer to him. 'Where I always felt at peace. If we had time, and the weather was nicer, I'd take you to the waterhole.'

'Never mind,' Leon says. 'Our swimmers are in the car, anyway.'

'I'm sure we could make do,' she teases.

Leon tips her face to his and kisses her, and she grasps him around the waist with her free arm as her lips respond to his. He runs his fingers through her hair, releasing the ponytail to let her tresses fly free as the rain returns.

A crack of thunder shudders through the rock and into their bodies, breaking their embrace.

'We better get going,' Laura suggests. 'I'm starving and we still have a long drive ahead.' Turning to the gorge she takes a final look at what was her refuge and her home before grasping Leon's hand and returning to the car.

Several hours later – having made their pitstop at the pub, where Laura was roundly questioned by locals about her new life in Sydney and her family in Bega – they arrive at the tiny town of Tuross Head.

Around 40 minutes from Bateman's Bay, it's nestled on a headland overlooking the Tasman Sea and is surrounded by two large lakes.

As Leon turns off the highway, Laura can understand why his mother, Sarina, wants to make this her new home. Rolling paddocks reach down to sparkling lakes on each side and they pull over beside the golf course to take photos of the ocean and lake vista.

After a quick rest, Sarina and Graham promptly whisk them off to The Pickled Octopus, a popular Thai and seafood restaurant overlooking Tuross Lake. As they watch the sun go down, Graham pops champagne and pours them all a glass. He stands and takes Sarina's hand.

'We have an announcement to make,' he says. 'We wanted to wait until you were here to tell you.' He turns to speak directly to Leon. 'I asked your mother to marry me and I'm delighted to say she said yes.'

There are hugs all round and applause from the other diners. A second bottle of champagne is delivered to the table and Laura whispers to Sarina, 'Congratulations. I'm so happy for you both.'

'Thank you, my dear,' she responds. 'And I hope that wedding bells may not be too far away for you and my gorgeous son. It's obvious how much he adores you.'

Laura smiles. She can picture a happy future with Leon, but they are young. They have time. For the moment, they are enjoying being in love.

Leon taps his glass and stands to make a toast. 'To Mum and Graham. May your life together be blessed and full of love.' His eyes lock on Laura's and he finishes with, 'To love!'

Laura, Graham and Sarina – and half the restaurant – return the toast.

After a calming, revitalising few days with Leon's family, it's Laura's turn to visit her loved ones.

When they arrive in Bega, Jeannie, Henry and Jack are waiting on the verandah to greet them as Ki jumps out of the car and runs around them barking in his excitement. Laura's mother embraces both of them and doesn't let her daughter go until they're seated at the kitchen table enjoying a cup of tea and an early lunch.

Leon is pestered with questions about his family and career before Jack and Henry give him and Ki a tour of their modest hobby farm. They have a small herd of beef cattle, some sheep, goats and chickens. Jeannie has a large veggie patch out the back, fenced in from the chooks and other wildlife, and Henry and Jack are converting the old milking shed into farm stay accommodation. Sarah came up with the idea, telling them this is a popular thing for city slickers to do and the Murrays are hoping it will provide some valuable extra income.

'Do you want to talk about it?' Laura's mother asks when they're alone in the house. 'How you *really* got those injuries?'

'I think we need some more tea first,' Laura declares, stacking plates in the cupboard. This is a conversation she's avoided, but the time has come.

'I haven't told you everything about what happened,' Laura starts as Jeannie cradles the cup in her hands, her eyes never leaving Laura's face.

'You know I've been working with Erica on the taskforce investigating missing women. Well, I can't divulge too much as it's sensitive operational information but as we made progress and started to put the pieces together about the people involved it got … complicated.' Perched at the table, Laura sips from her tea, trying to navigate the quagmire of the events of the last few weeks.

'The criminal network had insiders, and they shared information with them about us, the taskforce. I became a target and they managed to … to get me. I got these injuries trying to escape,' Laura's hands are shaking now as she relives being bundled into the car and waking up at the mercy of Cain Anderson and Karlie Wilson.

Jeannie's hands are now at her mouth, her eyes wide in shock as Laura's voice drops to a whisper. 'I was rescued by Erica and the team. Leon played a big part too. But Mum, the person behind the criminal group was a woman named Karlie Wilson.'

Laura scans Jeannie's face – notes the moment it registers.

'No. It can't be. Is she related to *him*? To Gary?'

'His sister. When she found out I was on the taskforce she made it her mission to get revenge. But she's gone now. Erica shot her. Killed her when they stormed the house they were holding me in. But that's not all. I told you I got these injuries trying to escape, well, I also …' Laura falters, her breathing quickening as the memories flood back. 'I killed two people, Mum. I had to. I didn't mean to or want to. I had to.' Overwhelmed by emotion, Laura holds back on telling her mother that one of the people was Simon, Erica's partner.

Jeannie rushes from her chair to her daughter's side, hugging her and letting the tears fall. 'My beautiful girl. You did what you had to. You don't need to say any more.'

When she has no tears left, Laura continues to cling to her mother like she did when she was little.

'I knew it was something serious,' her mother says. 'I told your father we should be with you. It's lucky Gary Wilson and his sister are dead. I'd hate to think what your father would do to them if they were both still alive.'

Laura lifts her head from her mother's shoulder. 'I took two lives, Mum. I had no choice, and I knew it could happen one day in my job but now it has … I'm struggling. I don't know if I can do this anymore but it's all I know.'

'I won't lie,' her mother says, 'your father and I have been so worried about you being a police officer. But give yourself time. Do the sessions with the counsellor and don't rush it. If you find you still can't put the uniform on, then leave. Remember what your Gran used to say: everything happens for a reason.'

Wiping away her own tears, Jeannie releases her daughter, clears the teapot and cups and brings out a bottle of sherry and two glasses. Laura gives her a look of disbelief – she's never seen a drop of alcohol pass her mother's lips.

'You're home and you're safe, and I want to hear about this beau of yours,' Jeannie says with a slight twinkle, changing the subject. 'That's worth a glass or two, don't you think? Now, are you in love with him?'

'Yes,' Laura says happily. 'I know we haven't been together long but it's like you and Dad. I think we were meant to be together.'

'Well, then, it shouldn't be too long before there's a ring on your finger,' Jeannie says with a laugh.

'We're not rushing into anything, but yes. One day, hopefully not too far away.'

When the men return, Leon has a weird expression on his face and asks Laura if she'd like to go for a walk. They leave Ki with her parents and stroll through the paddocks of lush grass that spread out before them like a never-ending expanse of green carpet. Bird calls fill the strange hush that's fallen between them.

'Okay, spill,' Laura blurts out at last. 'Did Dad and Granddad give you the third degree? They just can't help themselves.'

'No. They were great,' Leon replies, his hands fiddling with something in his pocket.

'So, what's up? You're acting very odd.'

As they reach the split rail fence of the main paddock and with grazing cattle as witnesses, Leon grasps her left hand in his as he drops to his knees before pulling out a ring. 'Laura Murray, will you do me the honour of becoming my wife?'

Laura stands, mouth open and shocked into silence.

'Um … a yes would be great at this point,' Leon mutters, his hands now trembling as he holds the ring out.

Laura drops to her knees and slides the engagement ring onto her finger. 'Yes. The answer is yes.' And the pair collapse onto the soft grass, laughing.

As they lie side by side, Laura holds the ring to the sky and turns it so the sun sparkles off the diamonds.

'You had me worried there for a minute,' he confesses.

'I just didn't expect it,' Laura admits. 'Not yet. But I'm happy, truly happy.'

'I asked your dad. I was so nervous. He was a little unsure too, and I get it. This is the first time we've even met in person.

But I told him you are the world to me, and when I thought I might lose you, all I could think about was how empty my life would be without you in it. If I've learned anything from what happened with dad and now with you, it's that every moment counts and I want to share every single one of them with you, Miss Murray. I want us to grow old together.'

Leon cups her face in his hands, and they kiss, soft and gentle, and full of the promise of their lives together.

After a celebratory dinner and drinks with her family, Laura and Leon are sitting on the verandah listening to the cows lowing and gazing at the stars. The Milky Way stretches out like a patchwork of shimmering lights in the sky. Resting her head on his shoulder, Laura sighs, the sound louder than she expected in the quiet of the night.

'Not having second thoughts already, are you?' Leon teases.

'No. I was just thinking ...'

'Uh, oh,' Leon jokes.

'I was telling Mum about what happened, well, most of what happened, and how the deaths of Cain and Simon have been taking a toll on me.'

'I thought you said the sessions with the psych were helping? Leon asks as he strokes her hair. When she doesn't respond, he tries to reassure her, 'You did what you had to. If you hadn't, who knows what may have happened? I couldn't bear it if I'd lost you.'

Lifting her head from his shoulder, Laura traces the worry lines around his eyes. 'But what if I can't get over it, Leon? Being a police officer is all I know.'

Taking her hand in his, Leon offers an unexpected solution, 'You said you always wanted to work with animals, with dogs. If you can't be on the frontline, maybe there's another alternative, without leaving the force.'

'Like what?'

'You won the Games, remember? You told me you could ask for another assignment and the taskforce was only a short-term secondment. You and Ki are amazing, why don't you share your skills with others? You could ask to become an instructor at the dog squad training centre.'

Laura stares at him, her mouth wide open. It's so simple, so sensible. Why didn't she think of it? 'Leon, that's brilliant. How long have you been hatching this plan?'

'Since you came home battered and broken. I know you love being a dog handler but if you can have a position that's safer but still gives you job satisfaction, I think you should take it.'

She reaches up and kisses him before snuggling back against the warmth of his body. 'I'll speak to the boss about it as soon as we're home.'

With that happy thought still in her mind, she finally collapses into bed. Their engagement helped to weaken her parents' usual strict rules, and they're allowed to share a room – Leon is snoring beside her and Ki is curled at their feet.

It's been a long, exhausting but wonderful day.

Swinging her feet over the ledge, Laura breathes in the familiar scents and listens to the sounds of home. The sun burns her scalp, as a light breeze lifts auburn tendrils of hair from her sweaty neck.

Heavy footsteps on the dry ground grow louder and she stands, wiping her hands on her jeans before facing the visitor.

'Hello, sweet thing' Gary smirks as he appears from the darkness of the trees and moves toward her. 'Did you miss me? I told you I wasn't the only one. Such a pity my sister didn't succeed.'

'Get away!' she yells. 'You're not real! You can't hurt me anymore!'

Gary caresses her arm before dragging her to him. 'I'm not going anywhere. You don't realise it, but you need me. You want me!'

'No, I don't!' Laura cries, twisting out of his grip. Grasping his arms, she pulls them hard behind his back and hauls him to the edge of the cliff. His screams echo through the gorge as Laura throws him off.

'*Now* I'm free!' she shouts after him as he falls.

'Laura, wake up!' Leon is holding her, shaking her shoulders. 'You were having a nightmare.'

She nestles into his chest as he wraps his arms around her. 'No, it wasn't a nightmare. It was a good dream. The best I've ever had.'

Kim Ulrick is an Australian crime and mystery author who lives in Tuross Head, a tiny town on the far south coast of New South Wales. In her first book, *Bad Country*, Kim showcased her talent for crafting chilling, authentic stories set against the natural beauty and eeriness of the Australian bush. *Bad People* is the sequel to *Bad Country* and the second instalment in the *Bad* crime series.

In 2024, Kim was awarded the Banjo Paterson Prize for her short story, *Shame the Stars*, and some of her short stories have been published internationally. Kim is a member of the Eurobodalla Writers, ACT Writers (Marion), and Queensland Writers.

Before becoming an author, Kim spent 30 years in the Australian Public Service, working with law enforcement agencies and national policy departments. Kim has a bachelor's degree in communication, majoring in journalism, and early in her career, she worked for a national daily newspaper.

Kim's stories are inspired by her life experiences. When she's not writing, she can be found hacking up the golf course, enjoying good wine, and walking on the beach with her family and her beloved Kelpie. You can subscribe to Kim's blog and access her short stories and other content at *www.kimulrickwriter.com*

Acknowledgements

In many ways, writing a second novel was easier, and in other ways, it was so much harder. You hone your craft the more you write, but your expectations, and those of others, are higher. As my evolution as a writer continued, my storyline went down a darker, more adult path.

Throughout this journey, my husband Shayne, my chief cheerleader and best friend, was by my side. Thank you, my love, I couldn't do this without you. So too were my children, Dylan and Lauren, who dealt with my many requests for advice about plots, characters and how to expand my social media presence. To my parents, John and Shirley, you had the privilege or should I say the pain, of putting up with my moods and me hogging the front room. To my sister Sonia, thank you for telling everyone in Far North Queensland and the many tourists who visit your gorgeous home to buy my books.

One person has been there through the highs and lows – the wonderful Sharon Phillips, who has the patience of a saint, an incredible eye for detail and a deep understanding of my characters. Thank you again, my friend, for your guidance. I hope the ride wasn't too rough for you this time.

A shout out to the crew from Eurobodalla Writers Authors Group, led by Karen Kentwell, who reviewed *Bad People* as the story unfolded and shared their critiques. This novel would not be as good as it is without you. In particular, thank you to Tracey Lee, one of the few people who read my entire manuscript and provided sage advice. As always, I have drawn on my online writing communities, Marion (ACT Writers) and the Queensland Writers Centre, as well as the Australian Writers Centre, for excellent content and inspiration. To C.H., you kept it real again, thank you.

Every author needs editors who can helicopter above the story, view the bigger picture while also diving into the minutiae of grammar and punctuation. Thank you to the Manuscript Agency for the brilliant manuscript assessment and to Pete Kempshall for your editing prowess.

Marketing books for most authors is the part we struggle with the most, and my sincere gratitude goes to the team at Elevatte Marketing in Malua Bay, who built me an awesome website and helped take my stories to a broader audience.

To Fiona Smith at Contempo Publishing, you once again had faith in me, and I am forever grateful for your support and the excellent service of your team.

I am blessed to be surrounded by some absolute legends in my local community – Stephanie, the Grahams, Helen, Bruce and the rest of my dog walking buddies inspire and support me (and provide some entertaining characters and storylines) as do the gorgeous Tuross Bluetits.

As an indie author, it can be almost impossible to convince big-name bookshops to stock your novel. My sincere appreciation to Jim and Carol, who sold *Bad Country* at my local Post Office, to Simone at the Moruya newsagency who did the same, and to Toscha at Moruya Books, Peter at the Book Cow in Canberra and Faith at The Woodland Collection bookshop in Bendigo. Please support local, independent bookshops; without them, indie authors cannot survive.

Finally, my absolute and heartfelt gratitude to you, the reader. For me, writing is first and foremost about storytelling. I endeavour to craft characters that are real, make you care about their fate and to weave plots that suck you in and won't let you go until the very end. I sincerely hope I did this, that you enjoyed *Bad People* and that I've repaid your faith in me. One last request, if you've read and hopefully liked *Bad People* and/or *Bad Country*, please post reviews on Amazon and Goodreads. It helps more than you can imagine.

Till next time.

Other books by Kim Ulrick

'In her debut novel, *Bad Country*, Kim Ulrick intertwines the chilling suspense of a serial killer on the loose with the haunting eeriness of the Australian bush. Set against the rugged beauty and inherent darkness of natural gorges, this YA Australian gothic will captivate readers. Wallaby Rock isn't just a setting – it's a character in its own right, a silent witness to the secrets that lurk in its shadows and in its past.'

- *Kate McCaffrey*, Australian author of *Destroying Avalon, In Ecstasy, Beautiful Monster, Crashing Down, Saving Jazz* and *Double Lives*.